2013 WRITING FROM INLANDIA

*Work of the Inlandia
Creative Writing Workshops*

AN INLANDIA INSTITUTE PUBLICATION

ISBN 978-0-9839575-3-9

2013 WRITING FROM INLANDIA
Work of the Inlandia Creative Writing Workshops

This publication is the end result of a three-season run of Inlandia Creative Writing Workshops held in four locations: Idyllwild, led by Jean Waggoner & Myra Dutton; Ontario, led by Charlotte Davidson; Palm Springs, led by Alaina Bixon and Maureen Alsop; and Riverside, led by Ruth Nolan and Mike Cluff.

The Creative Writing Workshops began in Riverside the summer months of 2008. In addition to the Riverside, Idyllwild, Palm Springs, and Ontario workshops, a workshop in Corona has just been established, led by Matt Nadelson. Look for their work in next year's anthology. The writers who participate in Inlandia's Creative Writing Workshops program are diverse in every sense of the word, and each piece is written in their own distinctive voice and style.

The Creative Writing Workshops are part of the Inlandia Institute's Literary Professional Development Program. The purpose of this core program is to foster creative writing and support the writers who live or work in and/or write about Inland Southern California.

APPRECIATION

This anthology would not exist without the talented and dedicated writers and workshop leaders who participate in Inlandia's Creative Writing Workshops Program, a sampling of whom appear here. It is only because of their hard work, and the time and dedication of Inlandia's Publications Committee members and volunteers, that this anthology was compiled, formatted, proofread, proofread again, submitted for review by the writers themselves, corrected, reviewed again, and then finally submitted for publication. Without that time and dedication we would have nothing to show for a year of good, productive writing—except, of course, the writing, which, thanks to all of them, you can now read here.

Inlandia's Creative Writing Workshops Program, related events, and annual publication of the Writing from Inlandia anthology are made possible by grants from the E. Rhodes and Leona B. Carpenter Foundation, the City of Riverside, and Poets & Writers Readings/Workshops Program, with particular thanks to the directors of their west coast office, Cheryl Klein and Jamie FitzGerald, and the James Irvine Foundation, funder of Poets & Writers Readings/Workshops Program. We also wish to thank Inlandia's countless individual donors and the readers who make this anthology worthwhile. All of these sources, in addition to the modest workshop registration fees, contribute to the production of this anthology.

We also wish to thank our host venues for allowing us to use their space to hold our workshops: the Smoke Tree Lounge in Palm Springs, the Riverside Public Library – Downtown, the Corona Public Library, the Idyllwild Public Library, and the Paul R. Williams Gallery in Ontario.

Inlandia is grateful for all of your support.

—Cati Porter, Executive Director

TABLE OF CONTENTS

2013 WRITING FROM INLANDIA

*Work of the Inlandia
Creative Writing Workshops*

Surveyors of Time

INLANDIA CREATIVE WRITING WORKSHOP — IDYLLWILD
LED BY JEAN WAGGONER & MYRA DUTTON

CONTRIBUTORS

Brutus Chieftain, Don Dietz, Myra Dutton,
Françoise Frigola, David Calvin Gogerty,
Richard M. Mozeleski, Jean Waggoner

Hijinks

Once upon a time, a 250-pound man wore a black unitard to a poetry reading.
He posed for pictures with a ripening sunflower,
hugged passersby, chased
a guinea fowl.
The gods were delighted with his hijinks.

After seeing one photo, his prison-guard brother
pronounced,
"You look like a pre-op transsexual."

Life hides some pleasures from turnkeys
preoccupied as they are with laws,
locks and sodomy,
contraband and cavity searches.

How can you ignore a bumble bee on a sunflower,
especially when it stings?

Once upon a time, a 250-pound man wore a black unitard to a poetry reading.
The gods were delighted.

Prayer to the Charismatic Poodle

Charismatic poodle, I can't predict
When you'll wake me
To bark at the Japanese jogger,
And recycling thieves.

That tail, that snout, those dewclaws!
Charismatic poodle you make me chuckle.
I accept my failings.
An overfed baying beatnik

chasing after a tiny dog and adventure.
I know your magic.
The way you nip my nightmares.
The way you bless my heartbeat.

Rasputnik poodle,
let's turn circles, cast spells,
tear flesh from trash. Piss
and roll around in it.

Charismatic poodle, keep me alive.
The way you capture my dreams.
The way you bless my heart.
I will snarl and howl gatekeeper.

The Peanut Wars

Prologue: June 2009

The journey from the desert was a pleasant drive traversing along mountain ridges winding from knoll to knoll. The vegetation changes from the dry desert to the mountain forest lush with oaks, pines and cedar trees.

After the hour drive up the mountain we found the cabin, our mountain hideaway for the next three months. We unpacked and got settled. Now the trip to Idyllwild for supplies and groceries. The minute we entered the market I noticed something different, barrels of peanuts and sunflower seeds. My curiosity got the best of me so I ask the clerk, "Why all the peanuts?" She replied, "You must be new to the area because everyone feeds the birds." We got our supply of the little morsels. Since we were going to feed the birds like everyone else we had to have a bag of bird seed as well.

Present: June 2013

We started the morning ritual by placing peanuts, whole and shelled, on the deck railing. We placed bird seed in a dish on the railing. With coffee in hand we rushed to our observation posts on the deck. We are ready! Let the Peanut War begin! The Blue Jays swoop first from an adjacent pine tree on the right, landing on the railing and bouncing from peanut to peanut until the perfect one is found. Taking off they head for home in a distant tree. Several more Jays are called to fetch their delectable morsels. The Jays become comfortable and compla-cent. They take lazy flights in and out of the landing zone. Wait! A new squawk is heard in a distant pine tree. It's the Acorn Woodpecker rallying the troupes to prepare to do battle with the Jays. Each bird shouldered its finest and most elegant battle armor. The Woodpeckers showed off their black tunics and white overalls wearing red berets on their heads. Meanwhile, the Steller Jays displayed the brilliant blue tunics with black accents along with their Pickelhaube helmets. Looking into the distance incoming "woodies" are spotted. The first of a wave of woodpeckers dives down from the right attacking one Jay with a swooping maneuver. The Jay is not intimidated at this first attack. The "woody" flies out to the left and makes a 180 degree turn. He is now in position to execute a much closer maneuver. Down he comes gaining speed he then pecks at the Jay maneuvering a close air attack. The Jay immediately flies to the left disappearing into the distant trees. "Woody" retreats to a perch in an adjacent tree. The war continues until the last whole peanut is taken.

Calm has now fallen over the battlefield. The Jays have their peanuts and now the "woodies" can swoop in landing to retrieve their much deserved bird seed after such a gallant campaign.

During this major confrontation the Chickadees, Juncos, and Nuthatches observed the war with curiosity and patience from nearby oak trees. They know their turn will come and they will be able to get their peanut tidbits and seeds. From the observation post a sharp eye must be kept so that the pesky squirrel doesn't invade the birds' territory and disturb the Peanut Wars.

The observer's coffee cup is empty now. It's time for breakfast and the day's activities. Later preparations must be made for the evening assault with a return to the battlefield.

Epilogue:

The many birds and squirrels that attempt to feed on the crushed peanuts and seeds that are served at this location have decided that the time has come to end this ridiculous war between the Woodpeckers and Stellar Jays.

The birds made a formal plea for help to the NSABS— National Security Agency, Bird Security Division. Responding to the request the BS Division enlisted the services of two fine negotiators, Sally and Don. An observation post was immediately established along with a demilitarized zone. The Jays were the first to be called to the peace table. Terms of the peace proposal were outlined. A fly zone was established so each side would have mutual respect for the territorial boundaries of the others providing harmony for all the bird

14

communities in the area.

The woodpeckers were next to be called to the negotiating table. The terms of the peace proposal were spelled out. After a short caucus the woodpeckers decided the terms were agreeable. The BS negotiators drafted the final peace accord consisting of a fly zone based around Longitude of 10.38333 and Latitude 43.71667 with variations of no more than a minute in any direction. The agreement included mutual respect and cultural understanding for all birds in the local community. All parties to the accord agreed that *peace and harmony shall be restored* to the local bird community. As a result of their success the BS negotiators have been asked to remain as peace keepers for the next three months.

The BS team must still be vigilantly aware of the squirrels frequent disrespect for the birds. The NSA is not able to intervene at this time because a squirrel squad (SS) program is not available. Until such time that a comprehensive SS plan is developed the squirrel behavior will go on unchecked.

Solitude

I was asked to take a group of Native American students from the desert on a Nature Hike on a day while volunteering at the Idyllwild Nature Center.

I gathered the 20 kids and we set out for the first stop on the hike. I was well prepared with notes in hand. I described the giant Ponderosa pine tree in front of us and included how to identify other kinds of pines. The next stop was a large cedar stump, which was a remnant of the logging era 75 to 100 years ago. I commented about the local forest being second growth and only about 75 years old. Continuing along I made stops to talk about the benefits of the dead snags and erosion. While stopped at Lily Creek the local flora and fauna was pointed out along with describing the delicate balance with water and the riparian plants including the precious Lemon Lily. The group moved on to the rock mortars, which were used by the local tribes. I made the statement that their ancestors, the Cahuilla, were the first snowbirds as they lived in the mountains during the summer and returned to the desert during the winter.

During the return to the Nature Center I reminded the group to be on the look out for various animals. Rechecking my notes I was satisfied that I covered all of my material. However, as I walked I noticed a young man about 10 years old shadowing me and matching me, step for step. He finally gathered the courage to ask what I saw while I hiked and what I thought about. Wow! What insights did this kid have? He caught me completely off balance. I had to do some quick thinking. I told him I looked for different animals, birds, and flowers. I observed rock formations, different trees and basically identified with nature. I believe he understood what I said from his reaction. I was so taken by this kid's question that it made me ponder and reflect on what I really feel when I hike. Later that day it hit me. Hiking was a time to reflect, to be in touch with your surroundings and nature. It was solitude.

Hiking Ernie Maxwell trail a couple days later this young man's question was still in the back of my mind. As a result my senses were more aroused, I began seeing, hearing and feeling more of my surroundings. Walking the trail I saw the lizards scampering here and there and squirrels foraging for nuts and acorns, Steller Jays, woodpeckers, Juncos and chickadees all going about their daily chores. Meanwhile, I noticed rocks and boulders forming interesting outcropping on the forest floor. How the pines, cedars and oak trees compete for space and reach toward the clear, bright blue sky. As I walk farther dead snags captured my eye because each one tells a different story. I am more aware of the sounds the different birds make. More captivating is the sound of the breeze as it makes its way through the forest. The red oaks leaves flutter in the breeze making only a simple whistle. The breeze rustling through the pine trees with their fine needles makes a loud roar that amplifies its strength to make a strong wind.

Stopping along the trail I admired nature's handy work of creating spectacular vistas, interesting collages and wonderful landscapes. A camera is always close by to record lasting memories of the walk. With my senses heightened, there is something else, a magic, a time for inspiration, for retrospect. It is a time to open the mind to be free to form ideas and think. Surrounding myself with nature while hiking gives birth to solitude. It's a zone for thought and reflection. This young man's question called my attention to my purpose for hiking. Yes, I found solitude!

The Green Man

While members of the community ventured to church in their Sunday best, I drove past with a smile, dressed in my down parka, warm pants, and hiking boots, en route to a temple in the forest. Upon arrival at the trailhead, my little dog, Uma, and I enthusiastically greeted the day. The mountain stood strong, in vigil, as if it had been waiting all night for our arrival, and the light from the rising sun vibrated with a finer essence than any found streaming through a stained glass rose window.

We walked alone under quiet, cerulean skies, no one to disturb our reverie. Ravens soared overhead, spiraling higher and higher until completely disappearing from sight. Uma snorted her way through rustling foxtail and buckwheat, uncovering the scent of those who had gone before us. At times the hair along her spine involuntarily rose into a mohawk, informing me that coyotes had recently glided up the granite slope to our left and bushwhacked down the mountainside to our right. Bevies of quail with multitudes of young scurried from one manzanita to another, the fathers bravely perched on rocks as lookouts, while flocks of small chickadees flitted rollercoaster-style through the branches of oaks and pines.

It was an autumn painted in overtones of grays and browns. A long drought had parched the Earth. Deciduous trees lay barren, and evergreens, dull as specters, darkened both sides of the trail. Unexpectedly, farther down the path on a rocky switchback, one we had traversed many times before, a glowing glen appeared. Its vibrant, emerald light saturated the air. Here a seasonal stream had gone underground, producing an otherworldly sense, perhaps, due to the subterranean aquifer. The green aura lingered, remaining inexplicably present, not vanishing in the blink of an eye, nor after analysis, but rather enveloping us in a liquid energy unlike anything we had experienced before, covering our bodies from head to toe in a verdant, flourishing essence—every molecule, luminescent.

Uma seemed fascinated, very still and quiet for so young a puppy. We had stepped over a threshold, through a looking glass, down a rabbit hole. Visions of turn-of-the-century English paintings came to mind with faeries dancing under beryl-lit skies, flying over verdantly hued bays. Then from some hidden place, I heard a whisper, a gentle, guiding insight that said, *"The Green Man. The Green Man is here,"* and revelation began to sink into my soul. The Green Man, Celtic God of Trees, of Light and Vision, of Wisdom and Word-lore! And it all came together—the trees, the memory of trees, my Druidic bloodline, speaking to me.

Church bells rang clearly in the village below, calling its parishioners to worship inside, but in this mystical glen, rapt in visionary power, listening to encoded messages from a different time, my prayers became praises of the infinite possibilities inherent in the natural world. I felt blessed, bathed in green, fully immersed in wonder, partly from this dimension, partly from another.

Thank You

Thank you, Sandy, for driving me nuts!

Thank you for deciding I will no longer be the one maintaining your computer.

You made me realize how, before each appointment, I had to prepare and brace myself for your sudden uncalled-for bursts of anger, for your refusal to do the simplest computer maintenance while complaining when the tiniest thing goes wrong, for your absolute refusal of manual backup while fearing to lose your client's data; and for deciding, without running any scans, that your computer was not infected when I suspected it was.

Within minutes of your email, I decided that from now on, I will choose my clients and only work with those I get along with, those who are truly willing to participate – be it in being tutored or in the maintenance of their computer—or those who, as so many do, decide that computer maintenance is beyond their skill or interest and let me do it on a regular basis.

I do not know who is maintaining your computer; certainly and hopefully, it is not you.

I do hope you will not end up in such a desperate situation as to have to call me. If you have to do so, in advance, I thank you for showing me that egos can be curved.

Thank you cancelling my afternoon visit of that day, then answering the invoice I emailed you with an angry diatribe.

One thing I will not thank you for: I already miss Tootsie, your dog.

FRANÇOISE FRIGOLA

Recipe for the Christmas Cookie Contest

[The invitation reads: "Early Christmas Gathering: Everyone is asked to bake their favorite cookies … Christmas cookies if you'd like, and bring about 2 dozen to share with everyone. Also bring along copies of your recipe, unless it is a family secret. (We were just going to share the cookies as dessert but Svetlana insisted we judge them as she hasn't won anything in a long time.)]

Search the Internet for recipes with a picture of cookies that look good and are as unusual as possible.

Read the recipe. Philadelphia cheese in sweet cookies does not sound too good. Instead plan on getting the Italian cream type stuff whose name you never remember.

Find out the recipe calls for "Biscuits de Reims" (Reims cookies: specialty of the French city of Reims.) Imagine a recipe requiring Portland, Maine cookies, if you were born and raised in California! Google "Biscuits de Reims." Discover that you can buy them just about anywhere … in France. Also discover that they are pink inside. Look on the Internet for a recipe for "Biscuits de Reims." Decide that this will be way too much work.

Brainstorm with yourself for several days about how to proceed without baking these <censored/bleep> "Biscuits de Reims" …

Decide which cookies would work to replace the "Biscuits de Reims," something crunchy and not as sweet as American cookies. Settle for "Petits Beurres," another French cookie which, fortunately, one can easily find in the USA.

But they are not pink! Rack your brain about how to make them pink without using chemical food coloring. Purchase two boxes of raspberries. Consider buying some red food coloring anyway, just in case, and then change your mind!

Empty the two boxes of raspberries in a small pan, add a tad of sugar and gently heat until you clearly have a nice juice. Strain, doing your best not to turn the top of your stove the color you want your cookies to be. Put the juice back in the small pan, add sugar, and bring back to a gentle boil. Taste and add more sugar. Keep an eye on it and stir often. When you are tired of watching and stirring because nothing happens, walk away, go to your computer to check your mail and start your daily backup.

Twenty minutes later, try not to hurt your head when you hit the ceiling because you have totally forgotten the raspberries on the stove. Arrive just in time before they burn. Looking at the contents, realize that it looks like a very dark raspberry jelly, which you could simply have bought. Discover that the goo at the bottom of your pan is no longer the delicious, sweet, healthy-colored mixture about which you had dreamed. Put your raspberry goo in the fridge and go to bed because what used to be raspberries is too hot to use now and it is already way after 11 PM.

Decide to play one game of Solitaire before going to bed. Lose the game, of course, quit, and do go to bed! No! You cannot go to bed yet because your cat is asking for food, and you suddenly realize you'd better clean up the cat litter boxes or you will pay a hefty price the next morning.

Wash your hands. Give a treat to the cat, hoping the other cat will not realize what is going on. Too late! Give treats to both cats in two separate rooms so they do not eat each other's food; hope they will not demand more food.

Brush your teeth and now go to bed for good. Realize that you have not turned on your heating blanket and you would instantly freeze, and definitely not sleep, if you dared get in bed now. Turn the blanket on and wait at least 20 minutes, so you have a warm bed and can turn the blanket off to avoid electromagnetic energy.

Next day—pull the raspberry goo and the "you just remembered it is called Mascarpone" out of the fridge, and let them warm up to room temperature. Peacefully look at the raspberry goo. Face the fact that it does not look that bad after all.

Try adding a tad of water, put it in the microwave for 10 seconds, and then attempt to mix. Taste it.

It is definitely gooey but tastes delicious and should work great. Realize that you will not have enough to make the two dozen cookies requested, but, so what? You have been improvising all along, so you will continue doing so. Put half of the Mascarpone and the raspberry goo in a bowl; add a tablespoon of powdered sugar, and mix well.

Now, switch your attention to the "Petits Beurres" cookies you are to reduce into powder. Read the recipe to see how many you need: it calls for one package! Great! Decide not to check the Internet to know how many cookies de Reims are in one package. *[Note: If you had checked the Internet, you would have learned that this famous cookie was created in 1681 and, until recently, was associated with Champagne and festive celebrations. You would have discovered that 12 cookies weigh 100 grams and that these cookies are also sold in powder form.]*

Start with one half of a package of "Petits Beurres", break them a tad, put them in a blender, and make a coarse powder. Add one-half of the "Petits Beurres" powder to the Mascarpone, raspberry goo, and sugar, and mix well. Notice that the proportions are perfect and you can easily make bite-size balls with your hands. Place them on parchment paper.

Unexpectedly, you end up with thirteen balls. Eat one to test. Enjoy, first the taste of the Mascarpone, and then feel the delicious raspberry flavor which stays in your mouth long after you swallow. Take notice, especially if you rinse your utensils in cold water that your bladder is requiring immediate attention! Take care of it while keeping your ears open. A series of very light Plonk … Plonk … Plonk also require your immediate attention. Look for the source. Water is dripping at the base of the toilet tank. Shut the toilet water off and flush the toilet again. Take care of all the water on the floor, and leave a rag for future drippings. Wash your hands.

Twelve more cookies to go!

In your oven, lightly roast two handfuls of pine nuts; set them aside to cool. Similarly, roast two handfuls of almonds. No need to keep your eyes riveted on the almonds, they take much longer to roast than the pine nuts. Just rush back to the kitchen when the smell of burning almonds makes you suddenly realize that … you did it again!!! Eliminate the few almonds that are not usable and let the others cool.

Decide that this second batch will be chocolate-based. Mix together about two tablespoons of powdered dark chocolate, two tablespoons of powdered sugar; then, add the Mascarpone. When the mixture is smooth, add some of the pine nuts. Mix and, with your hands, make bite-size balls; place them on the parchment paper with the other cookies.

Chop the almonds in small pieces and repeat the same operation as above with the almonds instead of the pine nuts. Be aware that since the roasted almonds are the same color as the chocolate, you cannot clearly see what you are doing and do not have a clue whether your mixture is ready. Mix more. Place the balls on the parchment paper in the fridge for two hours.

Prepare the chocolate: *guess how much you need to add,* put "some" Trader Joe's semi-sweet dark chocolate with approximately a tablespoon of half-and-half in the microwave oven for 20 seconds. Mix until you have a smooth paste.

Take a long bamboo skewer; place one of the raspberry goo balls at the pointed end of the skewer, making sure you do not push all the way through your hand and draw blood. Dip it in the chocolate.

Realize that your chocolate is way too thick. Add more half-and-half to the chocolate. Place it in the microwave oven for 10 seconds, mix well. This time it has the perfect consistency.

Place the skewer in a narrow high glass—cookies up, letting the chocolate cool off. Repeat for all the raspberry goo balls, putting about 6 of them per glass. Do the same with the pine nut balls and, while the chocolate is still warm, roll the ball in more pine nuts.

Realize that the recipe was totally wrong when it said to place the balls back in the fridge for 30 minutes and THEN roll them in colored sugar (which you have replaced with tiny rainbow sugar balls.) The rainbow sugar balls do not stick to the chocolate!

Turn on a small burner on the stove and gently rotate each ball over it to melt the chocolate … again. Only then, dip the cookie ball in the tiny rainbow sugar balls. While your pine nut cookies are still warm enough, sprinkle some tiny rainbow sugar balls on the top. Do not try to cover each cookie because you have almost run out of tiny rainbow sugar balls. Face the fact that you have run out of chocolate; melt more chocolate and half-and-half.

Switch to the almond balls and realize that the almond chunks are too big and the balls keep crumbling. For next time, take note to replace

24

the chopped almonds with almond powder. Do the best you can to hold the balls together while you dip them in the chocolate. Roll them on some sliced almonds and sprinkle a tad of tiny rainbow sugar balls on the top until you run out.

Carefully put the four glasses in the fridge. Place the almond ball, which is broken but did not crumble, down on a small piece of parchment paper; place it in the fridge with the others.

Eat the ball that crumbled. Realize you made way too much chocolate for your second batch. Put the chocolate in the fridge for now or anywhere away from your cats. Clean up the mess you made on your kitchen counter.

DAVID CALVIN GOGERTY

Dorcas

There were about thirty of us in the kindergarten class. Most of us were from middle class families, all except Dorcas. Dorcas came from a wealthy family that lived in a home on the local country club. Dorcas was an only child, thoroughly spoiled. She did not comprehend the meaning of no, and possibly had never even heard that word. She wanted to do only what she wanted to do, only when she wanted to do it, and either what she wanted to do or when she wanted to do it could change instantly. Dorcas was also blessed with a loud voice, which was heard frequently, regardless of what else was going on in the class.

Our kindergarten teacher was of the age of our grandparents, and had the disposition that any child could want his grandmother to have. She was patient and kind, and gently but firmly was able to keep Dorcas under some semblance of control. After a few months of that gentle guidance, Dorcas slowly started to get along with our other classmates, to participate in games and exercises with us, without trying to dominate the group. She became a friend, all be it, a friend with more than the usual idiosyncrasies. She conned her father into arranging a tour of her family's large dairy, a new experience for our group of children from suburbia.

After the spring vacation, Dorcas did not return to the kindergarten class. We missed her, but for several days nobody know where she was. One day, the kindergarten teacher told us that Dorcas will ill, and would be out of class for a while. This was in 1939, and sulfa and penicillin were not yet available. When a child became ill, it was not unusual for the illness to last for several weeks.

One day, the school principal came into our class with a lady that none of us had seen before. The lady was the mother of Dorcas. She told us that Dorcas had died from pneumonia the day before, and she wanted us to know how much Dorcas had missed us during her illness.

We all sat there in shocked silence for a few minutes. Then most of the students started to softly cry. The kindergarten teacher and

26

Dorcas's mother came and hugged each and every one of us. We cried harder.

For many of us, it was our first exposure to death. We all knew that our parents were older than we were, and that our grandparents were older than our parents, but we hadn't realized that our grandparents had been the grandchildren of their grandparents who were no longer with us. On Memorial Day we had visited the cemeteries where long ago relatives were buried, so we knew that life on earth was not of infinite duration. However, for most of us, this was our first actual meeting with death – the death of someone that we had grown to know and like. It had taken all of us awhile to like Dorcas in spite of her domineering ways. Eventually her domineering had become more than offset by her good humor and intelligence. Dorcas had taught us all to be less judgmental of others, to be more accepting of others' personality quirks. Her death taught us all of the impermanence of life, the value of friendships, and to cherish those friendships while you can.

Home

A house is not a home – does anybody remember the song or poem where that line came from? House and home can evoke very distinct emotions. A person or family well off financially may have more than one house. George Romney apparently has nine, and John McCain has three in San Diego alone. For each of these individuals and their families, which location would be considered to be their home?

In Idyllwild, there are numerous residents who have residences in other locations. According to the 2010 census, approximately 60% of the houses in Idyllwild are not occupied by full time residents. Of the part time residents, some are older, hoping to eventually retire in Idyllwild. Others have a second residence down the hill, either to the east or west, to escape the snows in the winters on the mountain, and to escape the summer heat on the flatlands. Which of the houses would they consider to be their home?

Home is defined by our emotions about a particular location, and not by the particular house. Home has to do more with the personal connections associated with a location, and in particular, with family and friends, which invoke a sense of belonging. That sense of belonging can be as part of a good environment or a bad environment; contrast the homes in Mark Twain's Tom Sawyer, Shakespeare's Macbeth, Eugene O'Neill's Long Days Journey Into Night, and Cormac McCarthy's Rio Grande trilogy.

Cormac McCarthy's trilogy is about several non-blood-related cowboys living and working on a ranch on the Texas – Mexico border. Although not related, they had many of the characteristics of a family. The ranch bunkhouse was their home, in that their lives were entwined with the lives of the rancher and the people on other nearby ranches and towns. In Macbeth, the protagonists, man and wife, though evil, were a family, in a house, and at the conclusion of the play, Macbeth grievously bemoans the death of his wife and his reason for living. Eugene O'Neill's account of the home he grew up in is of a dysfunctional family, whose ordeals he was trying to understand.

To me, home is the location with the greatest emotional

attachments in terms of family, friends, and community. We have all been in houses of varying degrees of beauty and opulence that did not impress us as being happy or unhappy. And some of us may have lived at times in houses and communities where we did not feel at home.

Robert Lewis Stevenson's life ended on an island in the Pacific, where he had made his final home. On his grave are the words "This be the verse you grave for me, Here he lies where he longed to be, Home is the sailor, home from the sea, and the hunter home from the hill".

Last Call

It's last call, the trumpet sounds
The moment has come, having made his rounds
Speaking to ears, to open hearts
To hungry souls in the distant parts
But its last call, the trumpets sound
Some too busy, others could card
The deceit of riches, of futile endeavor
This world's distractions are just too much to air

But the four horses cometh
White, red, black and pale
And seven trumpets sound off
Bringing sights of travail

Oh, some will yell "Stop this mad dream,
Give me a minute and I'll change my way,
I'll get it right
He is love, after all"

Oh yes
Yes he is

But this,
This is last call
This night's
Goodwill

People sleeping
Old man weeping
Missing lover
Mate for life

Dawn is coming
City bustling
His transfusion
For one more day

Children playing
Memories waning
A world long ago

Mate is missing
Night is coming
Dread of pain
Creeping on

Girding up
Breathing deeply
One more night
To miss her sweetly

Hearts Ache

Silent night
Quiet night
Peaceful light

Air is chill
Reflections still
This night's
Goodwill

People sleeping
Old man weeping
Missing lover
Mate for life

Dawn is coming
City bustling
His transfusion
For one more day

Children playing
Memories waning
A world long ago

Mate is missing
Night is coming
Dread of pain
Creeping on

Girding up
Breathing deeply
One more night

To miss her sweetly

RICHARD MOZELESKI

So Tired of Him

I don't want to see this guy any more, there is no more energy in me
for this relationship.
Everything is taken so seriously.
Too much intensity, the ying and the yang, the back and the forth, all
the highs and the lows.
All these emotional extremes, he's just worn me out. His "friends" list
is on one hand.
No wonders there.
His poor wife, an amazing commitment to a promise. His kid fortu-
nately had to stay or starve. The dog could get away, get out and take
a walk, but me, I was stuck with him.
He knows it all, just ask him. And yes, God loves you, but he (this
guy) has a plan for your life. Opinions, yep, his specialty. Nobody
does anything right, translated, "how he would do it".
After 50+ years of knowing him, you'd think he would change-So
since he won't, I don't want to see him anymore, I'm tired of him!
"Ah crap", he's here again this morning. Ouch, water is hot, razor
needs changing,
un-fog the mirror-
Good morning

Where Are You?

Good question
Have just landed on to the lake,
Having survived the river raft trip
Through 20+ years of rapids.
The lake is calm and reflective-
There is an outlet channel I can barley see at the other end
That's going in a different direction.
I can't see where, I can't see if it's smooth or rough.
I can't see if it's long or short,
But here on this lake, I can regain my strength,
I can regain my perspective,
I can try to repair some things in my boat,
And rebuild some trust and faith in my navigator
Who will take me on this trip
To a new frontier.

JEAN WAGGONER

Tone Poem: Crickets

Chirp, chirp, Chirp, chirp
Chirp, chirp, Chirp, chirp
A frenetic clamour,
crickets
sound steadily
against a swooshing wind.

Pulse, pulse, Pulse, pulse,
Pulse, pulse, Pulse, pulse,
an insistent chorus,
lovers
pump urgently
Against impending death.

Swoooooosh—slow death!
Swoooooosh—and now ...
Aeolus gathers his kin,
ruffles old cedars' ragged hair,
tickles tall oaks' curling leaves,
and *nudges* interior doors
Into ghostly gaping:
swoooooosh! He comes!

Chirp, chirp, Chirp, chirp
Chirp, chirp, Chirp, chirp
a leggy confidence,
insects
kick stubbornly,
although the swooshing builds.

Pulse, pulse—Pulse-swoosh!
Pulse, pulse—Pulse-swoosh!
Tympani and strings race to the death,

as Aeolus soars from ridge to ridge,
making freeway noise:
a passing of semis,
a rattling of gravel trucks,
a racing of cars
past speed-limit trailers;
all circling menace
and swooshing threat.

Chirp, chirp, Chirp, chirp
Chirp, chirp, Chirp, chirp
A door opens again,
A mammal lands on the roof.
Raccoon?   Cat?
Predator or prey?
Ears can't decode the thud.

Pulse, pulse, Pulse, pulse,
Pulse, pulse, Pulse, pulse,
a car slips downhill,
rubber on asphalt,
as crickets chirp defiance,
summer challenging fall:
Chirp, chirp, Chirp, chirp
Chirp, chirp, Swooooosh—so soon!
Chirp, chirp, Swooooosh—gone!

From a Smoke-Filled Daze

Forest ash invades our heads
sneaking up sinuses,
with aromas of damp pine,
cedar, oak, mulch and chaparral,
stirring deep sleep memories
into a stew of care and dream-
fragmentation, of steep snowy walks
to sequestered dormitories
full of friends, lovers, strangers,
and jumbles of others' clothes.

Smoke plays the kind antidote by
constricting airways and chests
with symptoms like a cold's;
tight throat, sniffles, sneezing,
smothering fire loss panic
with a stupefying calm,
evacuation stress with zombie peace,
fear with a relieved dumbfounded-ness;
a slow waltz of unpacking, re-connection,
and gratitude toward fire fighters.

Our town comes back to life and a
rhyme-form chorus fills our hearts:

We're back! We are safe!
Our homes have not gone up in flames!
Thank you, miracle of summer rain!
Firefighters, volunteers, our heroes, hooray!

Distances and Angles

INLANDIA CREATIVE WRITING WORKSHOP—ONTARIO
LED BY CHARLOTTE DAVIDSON

CONTRIBUTORS

Marie Griffiths, Marsha Schuh, David Stone

Poem for a Baby Boomer's Birthday

This night is not unlike so many others:
an indifferent moon plods along
her circular progress while untended hours
run delinquent, go missing—forever.

Come morning, her pale visage
will reappear from whence she started.
But I will have aged a year!

Decades have slipped away as slyly,
so just this once, I'll keep vigil,
shepherd hours, count my minutes,
pray they won't be snatched
by the slobbering jaws of Time.

Once upon a night, the pink glow
of a sea shell lamp banished all monsters
while I slept on a magic carpet, riding updrafts
of sweet dreams. The Tooth Fairy might flit
into my room and leave a dime beneath the pillow.

Now, more sinister sprites brazenly visit,
etch lines and splatter brown spots upon my face.
Wonder is I can still glimpse in my reflection
an imp with wide blue eyes and pigtails,
and can relive moments brightly when whole years
are dimmed, events erased as blackboards of their chalk.

Tonight, I am *so* loath to sleep and lose my year,
fearful of stepping closer to the precipice
of black abyss, fearful, too, of Yeats' beastie
slouching nearer yet to Palestine, portending end of days.
But maybe all of that is merely rumor!

For on such a soft spring night when half the earth
is giving birth, even The Celestial Watchman
might nod off. Millennia might pass undetected,
since, when He wakes, the cold dumb moon is in
her place, and our blue orb looks pretty much unchanged.

Judgment Day

Even Hitler had his Blondi.
High in the Alps at the Berghof,
a palsied hand sheathed in leather glove
stroked and petted her. When he whistled,
she came. He commanded S*itz!*
For such *ein braver Hund,* a treat.[1]

Even at *der Führerbunker* Blondi
was among the elect. That April
she had a litter of pure-bred Alsatian pups.
Such *ein braver Hund und gute Mutter.*

Russians almost at the door and doubting
the power of Himmler's capsules,
Hitler sorely needed a test subject.
Hier! *Komm*! He buried his face in her coat.
She gave him a wet kiss.
For such *ein braver Hund*, a treat.

So potent the cyanide,
Blondi died with barely a whimper.
Un-weaned pups carried up into garden sunlight
were dispatched.

On one side of the scales, *ein braver Hund*,
sacrificed, on the other, scores of walking
skeletons, tattered remnants of a race of men—
so easy to shed a tear for Blondi, harder
to grieve for the abstract dead in their millions.

Even today, *mein guter Mann und gute Frau*,
we would deny all men are brothers, absolve
ourselves of monstrous deeds, blame others.

43

Rather, on a fine day in June, let us
stand together *unter der Lindenbaum* ²
and bless the showers of cream-colored petals
crying softly on our gray heads.

¹ *Ein braver Hund* translates to "a good dog."
² Among Germanic peoples d*er Lindenbaum* or linden tree sym-
bolizes truth and justice. During the Middle Ages trials were often
held under its branches.

The Truth about Water Lilies

Standing before a prodigious canvas,
the old man combs fingers
through the white of his beard
and contemplates the task ahead.
Failing eyes no longer need
to see the pond
in his garden at Giverny.
He has memorized pink
and all the hues of blue and green.
Intimate with nymphaea,
he knows the long stem hidden
beneath pad and cupped blossom,
He is acquainted with the essence
of floating lotus.
Daubing palette oils, he brushes
elemental sky, water and flux of light,
each stroke a gesture of enlightenment
embedded in impasto.

Her virginal visit to NYC
and the girl has wandered
into a small room at MoMA.
Amazed as medieval rube
before cathedral altar, she sits
on the bench, transfixed
by the massive triptych.
For a moment she's transformed,
a nymph luxuriating in lapis
and cobalt, but stiletto heels
clicking across polished floorboards
and refined voices tête-á-tête
infiltrate gauzy veil of reverie.
Suddenly embarrassed,

an interloper poised to flee
she swears to memorize
each squiggle every blotch of color—
and, thereby, to understand.

Being

A box
A sticky carmel-coated moment
With prize inside

Time tells itself
A sketchy story
Yields kaleidoscopes

From water tales
Tiny treasures
Or junk prizes

Glass-jeweled rings
Flip books, puzzles
Magic tricks

Sometimes only riddles
Jokes left over
From second grade

True gift
Spills out only
As the box
Is tossed

Dandelion in the Drainpipe

Common flower
fringing dusty roads,
harmless gold
that children pluck,
open your mysteries
to birds and me,
your happy peers.

Spring's largess
strewn with lavish hand
scattering sunshine
in forgotten ways,
reveal in darkness
immanence of glory
that transforms
even gutters.

MARSHA SCHUH

Bathsheba

II Sam. 11:2 Then it happened one evening that David
arose from his bed and walked on the roof of the king's
house. And from the roof he saw a woman bathing,
and the woman [was] very beautiful to behold.

The king walks his terrace again tonight.
I feel his gaze, warming my flesh
when I begin the ritual beneath my canopy—
loose my hair, shake
the day's troubles from its tangles, stretch
toward the sky. Is it he who sighs
or the breeze in the cedars this evening
as my robe slips over the curve
of my shoulder and slides
its clinging folds from my back
over my thighs to the floor?

I cherish these few silent moments
of his enjoyment as his eyes
caress my body, so lately come
from the duties of my household.
Is it this fire that warms me or his desire
as I bathe in the light of its flames?

He thinks I do not know the depth
of his desire, but I have come to crave
the thrill of his passion, if only in my mind.
We keep this small fantasy alive, indulging
private pleasures, each in our own way.
We pretend, play at a touch we will never share.
What harm could come from this one pleasure,
safe in our secret thoughts?

The Anecdotalist's Daughter

Inspired by a news story by Susan Straight

Daddy loved Riverside.
He loved the smell of orange blossoms,
the palm trees, some with blonde fronds
that hung nearly to the ground
like girls drying their newly washed hair
down by the river.

He had yarns to tell about the days before any of us,
stories about the trees, the girls, the river, the way
he could walk from here to there to buy a beer.
People smiled when he wore his uniform
for it was 1943, and the country honored
its servicemen, who kept them safe
from godless little men in moustaches.
His heart was full of stories and he shared them,
one for every day until he ran out,
but his favorite was about his friend Sam.

Five dollars; imagine—five dollars for a beer,
and he was in uniform same as me. So I says
Hey, buddy, my beer was only one dollar.
Five dollars for him, the bartender said. Well sir,
I slapped a buck on the bar and looked him in the eye,
One beer, says I, and he had to give it to me. I slid
it over to that black man.
So we started talkin' and never stopped.

Sam told their story the day that Daddy died.

50

Today Was the Day Before

that moment in the library
when everything seemed the same
as we strolled through stacks
of unprinted conversations,
waiting for the perfect time
when you would realize
what I've been saying
all the while, only half-
believing, that what we'd planned
would have to be unwritten
one paragraph at a time
until we could read the book
from title page to epilog,
never skipping a page,
and find no trace
of what we thought
was written there.

A Dammed Life

"Dams, after all, are commonplace: we have all seen one."
—Joan Didion, "At the Dam"

Don't kill the beaver in my brain;
He thins the thickets in my thoughts
to dam the stimuli that strain
my creative vigor's onslaught.

My mental static's noise drives him
to gather sticks, stones, and mud
with paws and teeth to raise a rim
so fertile fish may swim the flood.

The power's in the murky pool.
I need its depth to swim and feed,
empowered by the miniscule
and magnificent waterweed.

At night I find my peace in-denned,
protected from coyote, bear,
and wolves who wish their guts distend
with my distracted brain as fare.

Don't kill the beaver in my brain.
I want to live a dammed life.

A Scorned Woman's Gift

A Response to Dana Gioia's "The Present"

Your arrogance glares brighter than my bow.
In time our bed will crack, bonehead.
The present that I gave you months ago,
its aim you miserly misread,
and blindly missed its knot's delight.
My elegant contrivance will ignite
the costly secret waiting still inside
to bring to light the justice you've denied.

Chicken 'n Dumplings

Aromatic steam hiss-pops the pot's vent.
I lift the lid to see herb-dusted dough-mounds,
shaped like cauliflower, drifting among chunks of chicken,
potatoes, translucent onion, breeching celery ribs,
and tiny thyme kayaks swirling in a turmeric-toned sea.

Raising my grandmother's wooden spoon, I taste the steel-cut flesh,
shuddering at the memory of opening the freezer door
to this chicken's nail-tipped talons,
splayed at the end of the fowl's frozen carcass.
I shiver at the lizard-like legs as if they were Godzilla's.

I had held the noose while my cousin severed the rooster's neck.
I jerked the head away as blood splattered
the grass encircling the slaughtering stump,
felt the blood soak beneath my bare feet
into the Lackawanna hill of my ancestral Pennsylvania home.

Now my face turns red from memories and the rising heat.
I drop the lid on the pot and flee out to my hand-me-down ten-speed.

I shift gears in fear, turning my head to check
for the ghost chicken's tire-piercing beak.

I peddle straight ahead of my nostrils,
tongue, and blood-stained fingers.

I want to drop out of sight
beyond the hills.

On Seeing the Cost of Time Change
for Roxy Heinrich

Old Ben saw too many francs
burning up in France's candle wax.
He trusted his vision.
He trusted his watch.

I am convinced of this.
I am certain of my fact.
One cannot be more certain of any fact.
I saw it with my own eyes ...
All the difficulty will be
in the first two or three days;
after which the reformation
will be as natural and easy
as the present irregularity,
for ce n'est que le premier pas qui coûte.

Frankly, old Ben didn't heed
his own aphorism's advice:
Instead of cursing the darkness, light a candle.
How could he know what he couldn't see
when he played with his watch?
A scientist of the Age of Reason,
he didn't know a chronobiologist.
His Junto never discussed the studies
showing traffic accidents increase
because they hadn't heard of a car.
It's hard to believe, Mr. Efficiency
didn't observe workplace injuries went up.
The good French wine must have blurred
his vision and slowed his heart,
or why else didn't he see the sharp increase
in heart attacks on the day they turned the clock.

But there's the catch, they didn't.
Ben's study group was just too small,
his hubris too large, his temperament
less regulated than his watch.
his letter to the editor of the *Paris Journal*
doubtless of his own perceptions.

I'd like to believe Old Ben would
have felt in his gut he was wrong
if he could have flown to France
on a jet and felt the lag in his eyes
for a day, in his head for two,
and all along his digestive tract
for nearly a month. But I think
Old Ben would have been sure
it was simply the food he could see.

He wrote the editor he needn't be paid
except with honor for his clever insight.

If Ben were still alive, I have no doubt
he'd be honored with a class action lawsuit.
The plaintiffs' counsel would surely quote
Poor Richard's Almanack to Mr. Franklin:
"Ignorance is not innocence but sin."
Or maybe he'd close with the French:
Ce n'est que le premier pas qui coûte.
This is only the first step that costs.

Riding the Flexible Flyer

When I was nine, I stretched to cover the red arrow
emblazing the sixty inches of our Flexible Flyer,
a trinity of clear lacquered birch slats
above Santa-red steel rails.

I'd stomped with pride my size-ten snow boots
through the crusted snow that covered
the long open slope of the Appalachian hill
that took a half a day to bail its hay.

Gripping each handle, I wiggled the rails free.
Releasing my hands, splaying my mittened fingers,
I smacked the glazed hill and thrust my body,
pressed to the sled, forward like a seal.

Fore flippers flapping so fast, I imagined
even the most blubbery bull could fly.
My sled sped with a sibilant hiss.
I retracted my flippers to handle my flight

past the brown blur of the thickets
of brush that bordered the field,
over the bump of the wagons' road,
across the strip between the gardens.

I counted the gray maple monarchal pillars, marking
the lawn's boundary line. I slowed as I crossed
the upper drive, curved past an island of leafless lilac,
and dipped the final stretch to the hemlock hedge.

Three feet into the cinder of the lower drive,
the sled halted in the grit and grime
of the Anthracite ash my father spread
to manage the ice and snow of our slippery drive.

Kosmos, Palms

INLANDIA CREATIVE WRITING WORKSHOP—PALM SPRINGS
LED BY MAUREEN ALSOP AND ALAINA BIXON

CONTRIBUTORS

Donna Buck, Anita Harmon

DONNA BUCK

The Standoff

It was during the standoff, really, that she realized that Ian was, well, a viable candidate for matrimony or what stands for that today. Love at first sight it was not, and a hackneyed phrase for such a triviality would have been beneath her anyway. Hell, she'd know him for years, if weekly purchases at the Book Nook and phone order confirmations counted as knowing. It was embarrassing, really, so unlike the flashy couples on the dating sites she refused to frequent (but knew about).

Nondescript—this was an understatement. Physically, that is. Tall, she guessed—she'd never really seen him standing, always as he was behind the counter, stooped over the computer checking book availabilities for her (she prided herself on reading the unusual and unobtainable), or processing payment. He was trim, well, no, thin actually, as was apparently the rest of him. Ian's arms had never lifted a weight and she was sure he had never run a mile (she was at the gym every morning after coffee). And his pallor was quintessential Brit: pale, SPF 100 for sure. Hair? What little of it there was barely covered his scalp, its color a barest brown, though not gray, fortunately. 5'10, she'd guessed, 150 if that, and she was at 5'3 easily as much.

He did have a lovely accent, modulated, precise, and a wry wit, so wry in fact, she'd often realize on her way home why something he'd said made her laugh suddenly, and wishing she'd still been at the Nook with an equally smart rejoinder.

Ian unfortunately came with a mother. An old mother. One who lived with him. Who worked in the store as well. The mother stared at her on her frequent visits. The father, you see, had passed and a few years back Ian had moved her in with him.

Was there ever a girl? A wife? Hard to tell, but just as hard to imagine. It wasn't that Ian was taciturn; he said little but what he did say was always just so. His eyes, a marvelous hazel (wasted on a man) twinkled, and they looked through you, past you, in you. He asked questions. He anticipated her interests. A year or so ago, he began to suggest books, a bit offhandedly, and they were always wonderful. He gave her the standard 20% discount but then had risen that to 25, because, he said, the books she wanted were often 'overstock'.

She wondered about that. How many of Maimonides' Guide for the Perplexed could there be floating around, for example?

But, it was indeed the standoff that brought it all forward. Five hours of entrapment for everyone in the strip mall, who had to wait it out, customers and merchants alike, along with the piercing bullhorns and the terrifying advance of the swat team and its black vehicle that afternoon-cum-evening. And that day, there were only the two of them in the Book Nook, which, considering the disarray of the shop and Ian's mild manner and unmerchantlike mien, was not surprising. But it would be a story for their children, if, what was she thinking—at her age—there ever were any. Well, their friends then.

War Bride

For a mother who suffered much

she was a war bride.
they urged her
to wed the "dear boy" soldier
who had suffered much
for all of us.
When he raced screaming from the theater,
home on leave
they urged her
to stay
for he had suffered much.

Later when she ran away
with an infant in her arms
they spurned her and drove her back—
her priest urged her just to pray.

She was an Aztec virgin
offered up to the god of war.
No one asked her if she would suffer much.
It was 1944.

ANITA HARMON

From a Portrait by Van Gough of Armand Roulin

The look of sadness first – or perhaps the look of blankness that steals over the eye if you stare at an object—say a garden chair—and think of something quite different—something that still haunts. For instance what Eloise said that morning at breakfast: *Of course I know you went to your sister behind my back. You couldn't bear her not to know our business* ... He drank his café au lait, tried to stare her down and this was what he might have thought staring at the garden chair: *She should show me more respect. Allow I have a life separate from hers.*

But even if the looking at garden chairs and thinking about one's resentful wife produces a look with a surface blankness, separate from the life underneath, this look could still be described as sad. As if life is passing by, untasted, unused, which is a state of affairs which produces its own sorrow—if more remote, less tangible than an unsympathetic wife.

It is no more easy to be a man than a woman, and Armand's cheeks are red from the sun at midday or from wine drunk in the vineyards with the other men—cheese and saucisson—with burst tomatoes no longer suitable for salad or seasonal peaches too bruised to be bottled, rolling on the earth between his knees. These red cheeks of Armand are second—underlying the sad eyes—signifying perhaps the rather damp look of the incipient alcoholic—the older, flush-cheeked man coming towards him on unsteady legs who will still be too proud to say: *It is all pointless because I am no longer loved.*

Between the Rocks at Joshua Tree

For some reason I think of Egypt.
The wind there they say
is the sound of the dead as they flow
between the stone hills, out
of the Sahara. Pharaohs, scribes
farmers, the diggers of wells
tall fathers shouting across fields
mothers singing.

This voice then, the only familiar
whistles itself up, then dies away.
The buzz of a fly, bore of a plane
cry of a bird. Silence is always
welcome.

The dead trail behind each one of us.
They have followed me here, stacked
high in the strata of rock, gusted in piles
of boulders, whispering in the Piñon.

Without these impediments
they could have no voice. Like wind
the dead must have their instruments
to claim our attention—their right
to haunt our movement to quiet places.

Haiku

Small mosses gather on the wall
Raise their spears at the winter sun

A pine cone rat-tats
On the Buddha hall roof
Delivers the moment

A Stellar's Jay
Rasps the winter evening
Smooth and quiet

Evening pools the Buddha Hall with ink
Candle shadows write stillness

Deep in the ivy
The way opens
In every small
But potent bird.

ANITA HARMON

Refugee Lament

that voice
that woman's
voice

calling out
for the recent
dead

strident
from the decks of ships
bearing strangers

who call across
to the
harbor wall

Where are we?

that voice that voice
crackling
like a wood stove

bed springs
leaned against a wall

hooting calling
through the pillars of trees
the shelves of foliage

the deserted farmhouse
rising to her throat

that voice
that woman's
voice

Humming Bird

Loneliness has
no antonym
worth a damn, unless
you count
being with other

people: little bright
iridescent birds,
very bold, immensely fast
needle the jasmine

the sky hurries
past with you gone

these delights
hurt

Slouching Toward Mt. Rubidoux Manor

INLANDIA CREATIVE WRITING WORKSHOP—RIVERSIDE
LED BY RUTH NOLAN AND MIKE CLUFF

CONTRIBUTORS

Celena Diana Bumpus, Michael J. Cluff,
Deenaz P. Coachbuilder, Carlos E. Cortés,
Laurel V. Cortés, Nan Friedley, Michelle Gonzalez,
Joan Koerper, Mike Sleboda, Frances J. Vasquez,
Mae Wagner

CELENA DIANA BUMPUS

NEW YEARS EVE 2012

El barrio, Riverside, CA

The syncopated music reverberated through my slight buzz in the hazy smoke filled room as I watched her dance, wildly, a phoenix reborn. Gone was the unsure, uncertain, indecisive woman I had known and watched for years. A sinuous wildcat, she danced alone. Slithering and slinking and shimmying her way around the other women. With precise rhythm, her steps calculated, but seemingly careless. Winding and twisting like a tornado, her hips swinging like a coming tsunami. Her hair falling from its clip.

71%

Riverside County, CA

New case
Same allegations
I can no longer
stoically receive these files
M hands me the docket
for my investigation
Tears cascade silently
down my face
before his hand leaves
the edge of the document
M begins the briefing
His voice is just
noise in the background
I'm way ahead of him
already deconstructing
what happened
M tells me what evidence we have
I ignore him dismissively
I already know
what I will discover
What they will tell me
What they need to tell me
I am the keeper of their grief
Someone has to remember
And I never forget

WHAT I LEAVE BEHIND

Riverside, CA

Tell me my beauty doesn't really matter
shapely forms are meaningless
Tell me my grace and poise wasn't what truly
drew you to me
It was my intellect that caught your attention
Tell me you saw me laughing with someone
and you wanted to share our mirth
You saw me speak casually to a stranger
and when the stranger left me he smiled
You saw me comfort someone who cried
and when I let them go *you felt* their sense of peace
Tell me you saw me out with my mother
and you admired my unconditional love
Tell me I intrigued you with my cultural support
because it made you feel a real sense of community
When you asked people about me
they shared my lessons
how I saw their strengths   future accomplishments
lives they never imagined for themselves
Tell me you've read some of my work
and it resonated deeply within
When I left an impression
you felt a sense of purpose
to bring positivity and motivation to others
Tell me not that I will be remembered
But that my lessons will be shared
For that which benefits all makes me immortal

ACT 4
(a poem in 7 scenes)
Love in the Inland Empire, CA

Scene 1
You radiated when we met
Perhaps that is why I thought you were
Apollo
Inconspicuous
No Hades
No Eros
And if I am not Psyche
Why do I dream of candles and betrayal?
Shrouded in darkness
It's no wonder I fear the night
Where are you now my sun god?

Scene 2
No I am not Psyche
Heck I'm not even Athena
I don't have any great insight
I'm just Diana
Empty hands held out
Fleet of foot
and fleeing the wreckage of our latest disaster

Scene 3
You said you'd give me time to think
Deduce where I was supposed to fit
You've turned the hourglass over
I stand alone in the wet sand
It was me who was really leaving
Me, who was supposed to have left
I hear the breakwaters in the distance
Why has Zephrys brought me to this lonely shore?

You call to me from the cliffs ahead
Since when were sirens ever male?

Scene 4
I fear the morning
Daydreams replacing nightmares
you are a holo-image
my hands can't grasp
Why can't touch your heart?
So where do we go from here?
You with your ties
Me with my doubts

Scene 5
You dream of flying
Once your protective embrace
grounded me in my sleep
Now I am drowning in your need
I prefer to watch you
when you are asleep
You don't want to know the truth
Behind my silent regard

Scene 6
You are starving
hungry
but don't want the food I offer
What is happening to us?
What the heck happened to us?
Hands that once cradled my heart
now squeeze my lungs

Finale
I am afraid to finish these thoughts
finish this poem
face those naked truths
These words scream to be released
I long to keep them silent

Nothing is real
if I don't speak it aloud
But my culture sometimes demands
loud noise
Besides, tact is relative

For Many Years
Seattle, WA to Riverside, CA

For many years
I thought of myself as a dolphin
laughing, brilliant and playful
through research
I discovered dolphins
were the only successful killers of sharks
besides humans
ramming their craniums
to crack their skulls
I was proud of my prize fish tanks
of small freshwater sharks
Until I evolved yet again
years of living in the desert
transforming me from dolphin to wildcat
reveling in my unpredictability
I embraced my dual nature
as all healthy Gemini women-children must
carefully and confidently gliding
silently through crowded rooms
widely noticed despite my soft steps
perhaps it is because of my echoing laughter
reminiscent of the Naiad I will always be

MICHAEL J. CLUFF

Mission Inn Piece # 1

October 27, 1948

Somewhere near the end
of October 1948
fate threw Priscilla Farmer
a wretched bit of eternal fate.

Having depended too long
on Larry Meagher's set of lies
from Santa Barbara he did drive
Priscilla onward will soulful sights.

To the famous Inn in Riverside
renown for the noveau riche
that graces the swimming pool
Larry promised Priscilla all joy.

For married they were to finally be
before his wife blew the deal
Priscilla, an heiress, had no sense
the perfect fish on Larry's reel.

However, she was an odd sort
jealous to a depthless degree
when the maid
flirted just a bit
Larry paid the heavy fee.

Priscilla always carried a rod
just part of the millionaire's job
Now Larry always sleeps very sound
and his life she then did rob.

This crime never made the news
on the Inn's protected lawns of green
forty million can quell all who talk
yet in hell, Priscilla hears those parrots squawk.

MICHAEL J. CLUFF

Mission Inn Piece # 2

February 13, 1952

Dear dead Ernestine Coyle
had to jump, it was no doubt,
off the Annex bridge
from the Inn
at its highest point
over Sixth Street
at around the stroke of seven
into the hard hood
of a large streamlined brown Buick
the master of this road.

Long lonely
and pursued
for seeing red
politically in the early thirties
she was being pulled to Washington
unwillingly to say
and affirm things she did not know
but others told her
she really did
and must.

A now single, divorced woman
is a prime target
for such hearings
she was told,
and that day
she had been replaced
in her law office
by a "more appropriate
suitable secretary type."

Life in a virulent vise
is no better
just as bitter
than any period
of uninterrupted sleep.

They said she finally
had a real smile
on her face
as she leaped
into the aura, arms, atmosphere
of a night
that judges none
under false fire and fulsome fumes.

Norco Poem #13—Pastor Morris Suchoutte

After fifteen years,
he still rants against the hills
and what they contain
atop.

It is the touchstone
of his daily
three piece suited existence,
the spice that makes
his "meatloaf on Monday
turtle soup on Tuesday
waffles on Wednesday etc."
unvaried diet
worthwhile.

"It is a sigh of Salem
sent west
by the blasphemers
of the Bible
the traditions
of the great nation
we refuse to become
are further corroded
by such Druidic beacons."

A son,
Gaylord,
sleeps
through all such
storms and tirades.

His daughter Blanche
feels the sermon

is silly
since a grin
on a pumpkin painting
emblazoned on a rock
just above her house
can't be all that evil
but maybe the upcoming earth-split
some parishioners predict
will prove
one or the other
side
righteous.

DEENAZ P. COACHBUILDER

I Have Forgotten You

After Pablo Naruda's "If You Forget Me"

At first we were planets
that collided and consumed
           each other.
I bit off a chunk of your shoulder,
              you sheared off my hair
and knotted my thighs.

I wore a rainbow ring
 around my finger.
  Work
  play
  love
  lust
    intertwined,
 tenderness
     anger,
   lacing together
   our laughter
  and our lives.

The years like moonbeams   the worms of the world.
                    cocooned us from

The years they wore away
our celestial cloak.
They sundered us
and flung us apart
you into the sky,
and
 buried
  the rest
of me.

I will forget you.
The way your voice   for   e
                    searched   m
when you entered the house
    at the end of a work-a-day world.

I will forget
the way I always knew those friends' names
you had predictably forgotten,
always read
the sudden knotting of your brow
the depths   of a frozen smile,
recognized
   your c o l o g n e,
            from   a f a r.

I have forgotten you,
forgotten you,
forgotten
you,
beyond the day
    I die.

The Green Hedge

Far from above, none of the sounds
of Mumbai city can be heard.
The setting sun drenches the tips
of balconied skyscrapers.
In the distance, crowded streets
border the landscape.
The dome of a mosque pierces the sun.

Through the glaze of dust and heat,
a quiet emerald oasis ascends.
Nine palms fringe an oval green lawn,
a cool breeze turns over the leaves
to their dark undersides,
while gulmohor boughs dally together
as they sway.

Here children chase each other,
shod in muddied designer shoes
across the manicured terrace
while maids watch hide-and-seek.
Pedigreed playmates barter video games
amid the scrap of roll and tease,
and scattered nursery rhymes,
as they bask in secure childhood.

From behind a green hedge
dark eyes watch the games.
Her only dress scarcely covers scarred knees.
Scabbed fingers tap longingly
in time with the infectious jingle of pop tunes.
Every day she sits on the outer side
of a gossamer hedge.

Spawn of an unschooled
vagrant woman who haunts
the crowded corner traffic stop
for spare change from captive cars,
she escapes each evening to
crouch down beside the emerald hedge.
She tells herself she doesn't care
when they don't call her to play.

Tomorrow's fantasy hovers quietly
beside her, where her shouts and laughter
might merge with theirs in a swirling whirl of happy cries
as quivering rainbows twine through their hair.

DEENAZ P. COACHBUILDER

The House of Loneliness

A swath of light hair falls across her brows.
Short and petite, straight nose and high cheek bones
frame a fine line of lips that slant
delicately down at the edges. Soft eyes,
a quiet voice with a clipped style of speech
muscular arms held stiffly beside her
when she strides along the street.

What do you do after work, I inquired.
Exercise at the Y, she replied.
And then? I hesitantly asked.
I go home, I'm tired.

She lives in a high ceilinged home
amidst seven acres of Port Orchard woodland
bought seven years ago.
Clear water from her own well
glints in a fine jug that rests
on a granite kitchen counter.
Two large dignified cats play in contentment,
encircling each other between the legs
of hand carved cherry wood furniture.
On most days she hears the blue jays squabbling
on the spacious hardwood deck.
Next summer she will plant five fruit trees
along her driveway.

Sunrise Against the Mist

sunrise
my brother's hand
curled around my finger

romping across the years
teenage conflict
then, he grew
taller than I
sibling rivalry turned
into shared secrets
bonds of the heart

but jealous waters
captured him

still
forever

my flaming youth tempered
to steely caution
burnished metal
into supple sandalwood
golden days etched
deep gray
a subtle sprinkle
of wisdom
the world's winter land

years of love
and life
extended
down the corridors
of time

Death parted the curtain
I entered with delight
to search for him
yearning for his
youthful embrace

the stars were smoothly silver
the winds most welcoming
those gentle spirits
drew aside
as I
hurried by

a faint glimpse
against the vast mists of space
drawing close
I called
and leapt toward
to touch
his well-remembered hand

he turned

but did not recognize me

DEENAZ P. COACHBUILDER

Yesterday

Yesterday I danced with revelry.
I slept and dreamt in silvered peace,
waking abruptly to a nightmare,
brackish, dense with pain,
devoid of reason.

I slept, whole, contented,
assured of family, fortunate in friendships,
awoke to treasures sundered,
husband, son, disconnecting
bonds of love and blood.

Hollow rooms
a necklace
of broken tears
moans escape a clenched heart
elusive dreams lurk
under flickering eyelids
a changed world.

Waste not this moment,
all is but ephemeral,
our signposts evaporating
into a shifting stream.

The nightingale sings
but for one night.

DEENAZ P. COACHBUILDER

The Stain

The refrains of the wedding shehnai
danced into the night,
he came in from the joyous celebrations
and took her with one thrust.
She did not have time
to take down her lush brown hair.
He did not awaken her sensuous lips
nor caress her maiden silk skin.
She scrubbed clean the stain from the marriage*sheets.
The stain on her heart remains.

Peach gold blossoms of the aged champak
scatter a welcoming net over the stone walk way.
Her child comes home today to celebrate
his twentieth birthday.
She blesses him with a garland
of marigolds around his slender neck,
a *tilla* of red ochre on his noble forehead.
She holds him close, born of that bitter sweet night.

The rain is full of tears tonight,
each drop a remembrance of that wedding night.
The cry of the shehnai reverberates in her head,
her gold raiments, her stained bed.
She soothes her burning heart, beyond regret,
the best is in her arms, forget, forget.

*marriage ... although decreasing in number, arranged marriages still exist
in India. In some, bride and groom are strangers on their wedding day

DEENAZ P. COACHBUILDER

A Paradise Lost

Why did they
labor across
on some destined
death march
over
the blinding walkway
leaving behind
shady moist mounds
of flowering azaleas,
these simple
chocolate brown earthworms,
answering
the Lorelei
of gleaming
cropped lawn,
deserting
their brethren's
quivering bodies
on the burning cement?

DEENAZ P. COACHBUILDER

The Language of Love

I have grown unaccustomed to the language of love.

Once I sang with the sweetness of my mother's lilt
and prowled great grasslands on tigered paws.
Once, my dreams were perfumed cobwebs,
thunder stalked my shadow,
eternity lay caught within my pores.

I do not dream anymore.

My world is the pleasure of professional success
journeys through the countries of the mind
ease in the company of old friends
sophisticated conversation and a sprinkle of light laughter.
Ask me the intricacies of correct stem and silver ware,
the labyrinthine maneuvers of city politicians,
the vagaries of the stock market. I know it all.
I am no Prufrock, I wear the bottoms of my trousers without a fold,
and am not leery of gently, inexorably, growing old.
I even recognize the plaintive call of the mourning dove,
the sweet perfume of new mown grass.
At night a pleasing solitude, all emotions enfold.

But you, woman, like a thunderbolt,
shattered this design.
Nothing of prediction, no pattern, remains.

Teach me how to hold your hand,
to touch the curl that rests against your face,
to learn again, forgotten words of innocent grace.

DEENAZ P. COACHBUILDER

Were You Lonely?

Were you lonely
> * Ahura Mazda
> before
> the Creation?

In the North
> the dark solitude of the night.
Beneath
> the vast expanse of time.
Movement
> as the sun skims across the firmament.
Harmony
> when the stars choose to sing.
The kingdom
> beyond the waters lay waiting to be born.

But no one to share a joke with
to scratch you in the middle of your back
to scorn,
> to praise.

Were you lonely?

---

*Ahura Mazda "Lord Wisdom," is the sole and supreme divinity of the
Zoroastrian faith, he who created the heavens and the earth.

CARLOS E. CORTÉS

Telephone Menu

Please listen carefully
because the menu has almost certainly changed
since the last time you called,
even if it was only thirty seconds ago.

If you want to proceed in English, press one.
In Spanish, press two.
In American Sign Language, press three.

If you want rapid service, press one.
If you've got plenty of time on your hands, press two.
If you're calling just for the fun of it, press eight.

If all of your siblings are straight, press one.
If not, press two.
If they don't particularly care,
please stay on the line.

If you are Catholic, press one.
If you are Protestant, press two.
If you are neither, please wait
and Jesús will be with you shortly.
At any time you may enter extension 666.

Don't worry.
You've only got fourteen more choices to make.
But if, at any time, you want to speak to one of our
Customer Service Representatives,
we're very sorry, but she's busy right now.

However, if you're an Elite Customer,
please enter your 64-digit password for prompt service
and Bubba in the Philippines

will be delighted to help.
Your call will be monitored to make certain
that you do not verbally abuse Bubba.

At the end of this call,
would you be willing to take a Customer Satisfaction Survey?
It only takes 42 minutes
and you'll receive 14 bonus points
on your way to the next level in our awards program.

Thank you.
We hope we've been of service
and look forward to hearing from you again,
even if you're still on the line when that time comes

CARLOS E. CORTÉS

The Candidate

My car was brand new, white and shining
but the bird, whoever he was, didn't seem to care.
I had to park a long way from the hotel, too far
    to walk there
    come back with a wet towel
    clean off the bird shit
    and get back in time to give my luncheon talk.
So I spit in my right hand
    wiped out the damn spot
    and headed for the men's room.

I would have made it if the candidate hadn't been there
    standing in the lobby
    greeting everyone
    eager
    smiling
    relentless
    not to be denied.
"Carlos it's great to see you."
I hid my hand behind my thigh
    to no avail.
Left hand slapping my shoulder.
Right hand grabbing mine
    firmly
    wetly
Then on to the next victim and the next and next
    loudly
    firmly
    wetly
While I went to the men's room to wash my hands, three times.

Five minutes later he's still smiling and passing the basket of dinner rolls.
I decline.

Essays

Today I received my social security check from the SSA.
Then I gave blood so the doctor could check my PSA.
After that I went to the airport where I was patted down
  by the TSA
to make certain I wasn't a threat to the USA.

Old

At 40 I qualified as old
under the Age Discrimination in Employment Act.

At 50 for membership in the AARP.
At 55 under the Older Americans Act.
At 62 for Social Security.
At 65 for Medicare.
At 70 for being required
   to take an eye test and written test
   to renew my California Driver's License.

Which raises a dilemma.
What happens if Congress or the Supreme Court
or the California State Legislature
should establish a new, higher threshold for Old
but I'm not there yet?
Does that make me Young again?

And what should I think now that
   the Transportation Security Administration
   has designated 75 as the new Old?
This means that at the airport
   I no longer have to take off my shoes
   before entering the body screening chamber,
   secure in the knowledge
      that my TSA Senior Discount guarantees
      my toes will be securely protected
      while some agent is zapping my genitals
      with what they reassuringly call
      the Millimeter Wave Detection.
Hm. What kinds of waves?
Hm. What are they detecting?

It's all too much.
I guess I'll just let somebody else worry about
whether or not I'm Old.
I'll just be.

CARLOS E. CORTÉS

Sonnet for Laurel

The shining face across the office floor
now greets me with a smile, a lilt, a sound.
A voice of welcome joy, I'll hear it more
each time I see the lovely friend I've found.

Our friendship grows as years go rolling by.
We talk, we laugh, we share, we look, we watch
our friendship changing as we're on the fly,
a friendship gently held we dare not botch.

Yet change it does, so effortless the trip
that neither notices the journey nor
the slow beginning of our time, we slip
into a love and life with so much more.

My friend remains, she'll be with me tonight.
Whatever comes our way, she'll make things right.

LAUREL V. CORTÉS

Sonnet for Carlos

The child slips through the light into the dark
Unwanted and rejected, he recedes
The gloom of winter's cold has left its mark
Yet all the while the urchin plants his seeds.

And in the spring surprising things occur
Around the corners of my mind he peeks
He smiles, cajoles and charms all in a blur
In playful games of youth he hides … and seeks.

Then summer comes. The child is tan and bold
And stronger, laughing, showing all his joy
No winter freeze will stop him as of old
This brilliant, effervescent Nature Boy.

I know the child. Around me and above
He grows within my heart. The child is Love.

LAUREL V. CORTÉS

A Memorable First Day of School

In 1968 our daughter Merrit was headed for her first day of school: kindergarten! We were brand-new to the neighborhood in downtown Riverside, California, so we had to go to the school Office first to finish registration. Then I saw her slip in late to her assigned classroom, beautiful and very shy, but determined. My heart was in my throat.

That evening at dinner, our student asked the burning and depressing question, "How many days do I have to go to school?" "See that man?" I responded, pointing to her bearded father. "He's getting a Ph.D. He's still going to school." The look on her face was priceless.

It was only at bedtime that my dolly said to me, "Mommy, I'm the only white kid in my class. Everybody else is a negro." I questioned her carefully to ensure that it was true.

I was aware, of course, that Riverside was the very first large school district in the country to voluntarily desegregate its public schools following the recent Supreme Court landmark decisions. The new law of the land aimed at achieving racial balance in every public school in the nation. In practical terms, this could involve busing white, black and Chicano students out of their neighborhoods to achieve balance in other schools.

The laws were loudly controversial, not only for those who had racial motivations for being unhappy, but also among mothers of all races who were simply afraid of their children spending all day outside of their own neighborhoods, and therefore out of their reach. In those days, people normally had one family car or none, and the man of the family usually took the car to work. That was the case in my own family.

Having moved three blocks away from Bryant Elementary School only a week or two before school started, we had not yet subscribed to either the morning Riverside Press or to the afternoon Riverside Enterprise. I did not realize that Bryant, being the smallest school in the district and having a small neighborhood population, was a chosen place to experiment on the structure, assessment and refinement of the process of desegregation. And I had no idea that the laws were being implemented so soon!

On the second day of school, Merrit and I went back into the Office at Bryant. "My daughter is the only white child in a class of black children," I began.

"Oh yes, well, we'll switch her out today."

"That's not my point. My question is this," I continued, "What kind of desegregation is this, bringing these students into an all-white school and putting them into all-black classes? That would seem to outrage the principle of desegregation."

They assured me that all new students were being held together in several classrooms, only to be tested and placed at their appropriate class levels. Merrit, too, would be tested and placed into one of the two kindergarten classes that day. And so she was.

Within a few days, black and Chicano students at Bryant School were interspersed among the classrooms— with the expected level of external pressure and protest, but with no incident whatsoever within the school. And our daughter, Merrit Winters, now a 3rd grade teacher in Temecula, was a participant in a rare moment of history, giving her indeed a most memorable first day of school.

LAUREL V. CORTÉS

He's Gone

Then he was gone, the range's finest guest.
He ruled his land for only thirty years.
The lure of gold and quiet brought him West
And left his mother aching and in tears.
But when the mines played out with paltry gains
He chose the honest labor of the plains.

The Civil War had taught him strategies
To deal with hardships on the cattle drive
While trying hard to cope with tragedies
And guilt he felt that he was still alive.
He ranched with fellow soldiers from both sides
Who sought the same forgiveness on their rides.

His playground was two thousand miles in length
A pathless parch of cactus, sand and stone
He worked with youthful health and country strength
Until one day he woke up with a moan,
Stove up with aching back, stiff as a board
And wrong-healed broken bones he had ignored.

But rich folks had already bought the plains
They put up wire, and water soon was sold!
The cattle drives were halted, since the trains
Could take cows, fat and tender, not too old
Up to Chicago's packing plant to sell.
All gone, the life our hero loved so well.

My Dad was born a cowboy, this is true!
He worked from childhood on, first light to last.
But he was just an echo—that he knew—
Of nature's pure anarchists of the past:

The nineteenth-century cowman in his prime
Who fired imaginations for all-time.

And Daddy was a cowboy till the end.
He died with his horse Nellie on his mind;
He said he'd never found a better friend.
When riding in Wyoming they would find
The quiet, private time they always craved
To offset all the trials they had braved.

Reunion

It was the kind of evening once familiar, but no more. A taste of salt and the softness of the air are signs that you are near the ocean, at least to those of us who come back to the coast.

It was La Jolla in 1967. My good friends had invited me to their home for the weekend, and I knew that the Friday night party was already under way.

Their home, set above La Jolla Shores, was modest by La Jolla standards, except for one thing: the living room featured wraparound windows that provided an incomparable panorama of the ocean and coastline. The house was set out on a promontory from which the land lay back out of sight, affording a mesmerizing view both north toward Del Mar and following the curve of the cliffs past the La Jolla Beach and Tennis Club to the south.

But I had come to see the new house, the glass house on the pristine beach below. There was a four-seat funicular gliding on a track down the cliffs to the owner's hidden private cove, and as it slowly carried me down to my destination I was struck once again by the excruciating beauty of the place, and by the many memories it evoked.

Once on the beach, I took off my shoes and walked toward the music and laughter into the magnificent round glass edifice built against the cliff, with angles and prisms everywhere; a sparkling centerpiece to all that awesome nature could provide.

When I stopped to focus on the people inside the house instead of the structure itself, I was astonished to recognize that all of the favorite people of my own life were in attendance. My Mom and Dad, all seven of my siblings, friends from Carlsbad and La Jolla, my college roommates, two of my favorite teachers from San Diego State, colleagues from Riverside, even my husband and two babies were there. How did they get there?

Who was there? Everyone who had ever loved me; there was no one missing.

Overwhelmed by emotion, I stepped back out of the glass

house and onto the secluded beach. There was a stillness outside that is rare at the coast: no breeze, no sound except the muted laughter from inside the showcase. But now there was a louder sound, like rumbling thunder. I turned slowly with an inexplicable feeling of dread.

What I saw sent me into an unnatural rage. The waves had receded, just in the few moments I had been inside, and there were fish floundering and flopping around on the wet ground. Tsunami! I searched for another sign, and there it was: The thick, black mark rising above the horizon, all along the discernible waterline. Tsunami!

Instinctively I ran back to the funicular, intent on escape, but it was parked back at the top of the cliff. I stared up at the house high on the hill, back to the surrounding prison, and then out to the fast-receding water. "Fish are jumpin', and the cotton is high," I caught myself singing. The long, unbroken line on the western horizon was thicker now, and I stood still for a moment to marvel at the sight: the colors of the moonlit sky, the sparkling wet sand, the fish, the kelp, the fatal wave …

I pressed the button to bring the funicular down the track. My mind was racing: did I hear my babies cry? Only four seats and so little time!

Hurrying to get my husband and children, I glanced back nervously at the looming darkness. But when, through the window glass, I saw my mother, my best friend, and two of my sisters laughing together, I stopped. Looking over at the funicular car—now waiting at the bottom of the cliff—I sighed, then with a rueful smile I moved calmly to the entrance of the glorious glass house.

Inside, without a word I kissed my husband and joined my beloved companions. I was handed a shot of tequila "con limón y sin sal," by someone who knew me very well, for that was always my drink of choice in a crowd. Very soon I was joining in the laughter, hugging my babies, and thinking, "This is the best, being with the people I love and who love me. I'm so happy to see everyone again."

NAN FRIEDLEY

Moving to the IE

It was my biggest move.
The one that required a Mayflower truck.
Between the garage sale and
What I gave away,
My life filled
Only a third of the moving van.
The day the movers came
Was the day my house sold.
I signed documents on boxes
Taped and labeled with contents.
Boxes that contained memories of
Where I had been,
Bits of my past carefully wrapped
In newspaper to protect them,
Keep them safe from
An uncertain future.

Pioneer

It was 1985 and I had just arrived.
Rancho Cucamonga was still just Cucamonga.
There wasn't much of that
At the corner of Haven and Baseline
Nothing between my apartment and Mount Baldy.
I'd never heard of winds called Santa Anas.
Winds that swept dust through every
Crack or crevice of window and doorframe
Coating my life with a veil of secrecy
Leaving a brown film on tables for me
To trace, "Help, I don't belong here".

Coyotes howled nightly in the distance.
Their glowing eyes, staring, challenging,
Telling me I was the invader
That I was not welcome in their land.
A land that was foreign to me
And yet had become my home.

A scaly lizard took refuge in my kitchen
Daily I chased it with a broom
But the creature prevailed behind the frig
Wanting to be included
Hoping to be a fellow pioneer
In my frontier adventure.

Ramp Work

Closed intermittently thru 8/31/2014
That is the sign posted on Arlington Avenue.
Cement barricades divert traffic so that
Three lanes become two,
Then, two lanes become one.
Now I avoid Arlington.

Instead I use Central Avenue
Narrow, rugged terrain
The sign here says closed
Intermittently thru 8/31/2014
Merge quickly, slow lane exits
Stuck getting off at Arlington anyway.
Now I avoid Central.

So I use 14th Street.
The bridge is being renovated
Only one lane going in each direction
Leaving me to wait
Through three red lights
Sign posted
Closed intermittently thru 8/31/2014.

Can't wait until 8/31/2014.
My life will suddenly
Become less complicated.

Huntington Beach Day (a sestina)

It's time for a day at the beach.
A lazy Tuesday in the middle of June.
Pack up the car, head west on the 91 and 55, south.
Morning fog lifts around noon.
Surfers packing up from their last rides of the day.
Parking spaces vacated for those seeking a bronze glow.

Slather on the Coppertone to achieve that summer glow.
Sun worshippers wedge themselves into the sandy beach.
Ready to relish the soothing warmth of the day.
But the sun is not at its peak yet in June.
Best sun hours are between 1:00 and 3:00, but get here by noon.
Be careful, the UV rays can be strong in the CA south.

Those in the northern reaches, drive south.
Leaving the cold "temps" and gray skies for the sun's glow.
Open up the Penguin cooler, pop the Diet Coke top, it's almost noon.
Grab a PB&J, munch some Doritos, picnic style beach.
Shaking off the stress for a relaxing day in June.
That trashy novel you've waited to read … today's the day.

Too hot to read, too hot to sleep in the middle of the day.
Take a walk, let the waves chase your toes … heading south.
Junior lifeguards in training, learning the ropes this June.
Sailboats careening the waves, sails all aglow.
Seashells scatter, the tide sweeps slimy seaweed onto the beach.
It's almost 3:00. Can't believe I've been here since noon.

I left my worries behind at noon.
Better jump in the waves, benefit from what's left of the day.
Enjoy the smell of the sea and the sounds of the beach

Before heading home, driving northeast from the south.
My skin feels hot, maybe too much glow.
I usually burn in August, rarely in June.

Is global warming the culprit of my sunburn in June?
Or is it because I haven't applied sunscreen since noon?
It will just let others know I have a beach day glow.
Shake out the beach towel, pack up for the day.
Driving the car north, wishing I was staying south
Longing for the next day spent at the beach.

Maybe before June ends, I can plan another day.
Plan to leave early, arrive before noon on my next trip to the south.
By then, I'll need to feel the glow of another sunny day at the beach.

NAN FRIEDLEY

Not in Kansas Anymore

It seemed the end was near, but I hoped that my last day on Earth wouldn't be in a single-wide trailer with 30, 3rd graders. Santa Ana winds roared through the Fontana Pass, slapping telephone lines onto the roof of our portable classroom. Looking out one of our three windows, tumbleweeds rolled past at breakneck speed. Visible dust clouded the view. The temporary building swayed side to side like a 747 in turbulence. Increasingly I felt as if we would roll over into the vacant lot next door and just keep going.

A student on the back row raised his hand. "May I go to the bathroom?" I looked at him with my most convincing "Are you serious?" teacher face, but I could tell from his jiggling legs it was an emergency call. I nodded my permission. The nearest bathroom for boys was by the office so it required a walk on the wild, windy side. I met him at the door leading the way to winds like those that transported Dorothy. We both reached for the knob, turning it with apprehension. Just then, a gust of wind yanked the doorknob out of our grip slamming it against the classroom exterior wall. I'm not sure if the student still had to use the bathroom, but now I did.

BI in the IE

Dedicated to the Brandin' Iron, San Bernardino, CA

Neon beer signs light my way
Same guys playing pool by the door
You can see me here every Thursday
Same cowboys on stools by the dance floor.

Same guys playing pool by the door
Wearing my Justin boots, wearing my straw hat
Same cowboys on stools by the dance floor
Do these jeans make me look fat?

Wearing my Justin boots, wearing my straw hat
Dancers moving in a gyrating line
Do these jeans make me look fat?
I'll look better if you drink some wine.

Dancers moving in a gyrating line
Birthday cakes and shots for all
I'll look better if you drink more wine.
Order one more before last call.

Birthday cakes and shots for all
You can see me here every Thursday
Order one more before last call.
Neon beer signs light my way,.

Brevee Collection

Brillo
Pillow
Can't get to sleep
Dull bed
Full head
Just count the sheep.

Farmer
Charmer
Tiller of land
Sowing
Growing
Help from God's hand.

Toffee
Coffee
Jolt for the day
Wake me
Break free
Caffeine my way.

Teacher
Preacher
Leader of class
Learning
Yearning
Some say, "I'll pass."

Slender
Bender
Cirque Du Soleil
Twirling
Swirling
Can't look away.

Bombers
Glommers
Lust for some press.
Hated
Sated
Leave a big mess.

Family Anomaly

We all have something.
Some have a big nose like Uncle Bill
Some have curly hair like Grandma
Others a birth mark.

My grandfather on my dad's side had it
Not sure it went back farther than that
But it seems to have stopped with me.
The distinction of webbed toes.

Two on the right foot.
Not the little piggy who went to market
But the one who stayed home and
The one who had roast beef.

It doesn't really improve my swimming skills.
You'd think I would just swim in circles.
Hey, Donald Duck could swim
Circles around me any day.

Having webbed toes
Makes pedicures challenging
Fitting dividers
Elicits curious looks from the Happy Nails staff.

Oddly enough, I don't try to keep them a secret
I proudly wear flip-flops
Displaying
My freakish toes to anyone.

I've tried wearing toe rings
But my webbed feet just laugh at me

They reject the adornment
Suggesting I try ankle bracelets.

When my daughter was born
I counted all her fingers
And was happy to see that she had
Ten long, separate toes.

Band-Aids

A Sestina

A skinned knee, scraped elbow, a cut
Cover it with a Superman band-aid
When I was three, band-aids made me forget
Disguised the disfiguring mark
A badge to show that I survived a wound
A reminder that I'm not invincible.

And I'm certainly not invincible
Sometimes a disapproving look makes a cut
So deep it leaves an unbearable wound
Put on a brave Batman band-aid
But underneath, the face of disappointment left its mark
One I didn't forget.

I wish there was a band-aid that made me forget
Not dwell on my failures, focus on successes, could I be invincible?
To be remembered, leaving an indelible mark
On the world, that I've made the cut
With my Transformer band-aid
I've been there, made a difference, healed a wound.

Band-aids don't hide a wound
Made by those who ridicule, demean, leaving me to forget
That I must put on a happy face band-aid
And even if I'm not, try to be invincible
It's time to cut
My losses, begin again at a new mark.

Loneliness levels a secret mark
An emptiness that creates a gaping wound
Hidden, unspoken, a measured cut
From feeling apart from someone beyond me, seeking to forget
That I'm far from invincible
Apply a beige, flesh-toned band-aid.

Some days I need a giant SuperHero band-aid.
All the memories have left a collective mark
From days when I wasn't invincible.
Days that I ripped off the band-aid and picked at the wound
So much to remember, much more to forget
Some days even a giant SuperHero band-aid doesn't cover the cut.

Time to peel off the band-aid, inspect the cut
Leaving me an invincible wannabe, lessons learned I won't forget
A scar, a mark, a constant reminder of a past wound.

It's Over

How can a love just fade and slip away?
Or was it never really there at all?
In the end, there was nothing left to say.

We were young, waiting for real lives to start.
Launching careers, full of promise and hope.
Is that when love began to fall apart?

A wedge started to chip the love away.
The lure of work and money took its toll.
Success in his work kept our love at bay.

"I won't be home for dinner", I heard.
"I'm working late tonight," I sighed.
Chips of love fell away without a word.

Raging temper flared, he swore and he screamed.
A kicked in door, missiles of anger released.
More bits of love broken off so it seemed.

We talked the talk to mend what we had.
He said he would try, I said I would too.
But our love was broken, battered, and sad.

I do believe there was a love we shared.
Now emptiness at the end of the day.
Tired of feeling alone, hopeless, and scared.
At the end, there was nothing left to say.

MICHELLE GONZALEZ

House on Audubon

It was a rental
And the first place
We hung pictures
And window shades
First place I made
Meatloaf and mashed potatoes,
Laughing and talking
With company
At the dinner table.

First place where we
Fought till one AM
Trying not to go to bed
With malice on our minds.
And the first place where
We made up at two AM
And slept in till eleven AM.

It's also where we slept
In the narrow living room
One boiling summer night
Hoping the small a/c
Would keep us cool.

Where the neighbor's dog barked
Each time we walked by
The sliding back door,
And we had an impromptu yard sale
One Saturday afternoon
Making only five dollars.

It's the place where the porch light
Went out on Thanksgiving,
Later the car was broken into
And the radio stolen.
It's surprisingly the place
I was sad to leave
When we bought
Our own home.

The Dessert

"This is excellent, MJ!" exclaimed Robin. "It's like a vegetarian moussaka soup. Or a gazpacho. Let me see, I'm tasting eggplant and tomatoes, obviously, and onions ..."

"Green peppers and zucchini," Dean added, inspecting his spoon before lifting it to his mouth.

"The spices are wonderful! They just blossom on my palate like a magnolia in Georgia," said Robin in her Southern drawl. "It's so tender ..."

"That's because I sautéed the onions first in olive oil. Then after they were glistening, I added the cubes of eggplant and spices and continued to sauté them together until the eggplant started to soften and glow like a frosted window," I explained. "That was my signal to add the chopped zucchini and water. After about an hour, I added the Italian tomatoes and green peppers and let it all simmer for another hour or so. I just cooked it slowly until it was done, whenever that was," I laughed. "I let it cool down, then threw it in the blender and put it in the refrigerator. When it came time to serve dinner, I topped each portion with a touch of shredded cheddar, a dab of sour cream, and mint.

"To me, it was a zinger today and way too sizzling for a hot meal even though we are at the beach. This meal is equally tasty either chilled or hot."

"Oh, I agree on both counts. It *was* a scorcher today! And this meal is just perfect. What recipe did you use?" Robin inquired.

"You know me. I didn't use a recipe. Each meal evolves. I never know how it will turn out!"

"I have to say, this may be one of your best meals yet, MJ" complimented Dean.

"Thanks for bringing the homemade pumpernickel bread," I added. "It is the perfect complement."

We savored the entree listening to ocean waves gently lapping up onto the beach, sipping the last of our mint juleps, sharing stories and silence, completely comfortable with each others' company.

Dishes cleared, I retired to the kitchen to prepare the dessert, an extraordinary treat my mother served on rare occasions after she cooked a meal with rice. Growing up in a meat, potatoes, and salad Midwest home, my mother only cooked rice when she made chow mein, the singular Oriental meal that graced our table. Spaghetti was her nod to Italian cuisine until Stouffer's made family sized portions of frozen lasagna. Mexican and Greek foods were unheard of in our home. Simply put, Mother never learned how to cook such "exotic" meals. On the other hand, Mother's rice pudding was the best I've ever tasted. Only occasionally am I able to mimic it, although I use her hand written recipe and follow it explicitly.

But on that sultry summer day, using the oven to bake rice pudding was out of the question. Instead, I put together the dessert Mom made us on those special days after chow mein.

Taking the casserole dish of cooked Basmati rice out of the refrigerator I crumbled the chilled rice into individual Chinese porcelain bowls, and sprinkled it with brown sugar, cinnamon, and pinches of clove and nutmeg. Instead of cow's milk, I slowly poured rice milk on top, watching it tumble and swirl into rice inhabited reefs, each drop forming a glistening fractal of love.

Topping each bowl with small sprigs of mint, I transferred them to my parents' hand-tooled Farberware aluminum serving tray, surrounding a fresh pitcher of iced Darjeeling tea, and added spoons and cotton cloth napkins. "Here we go Mom," I said, smiling as much with my heart as my lips. "Your rice dessert looks so pretty! You would just love it. I love *you*, Mom," I whispered to the wind, knowing it would carry the message two-thousand miles to her soul.

"What's this?" Dean asked as I served him. "A very nice presentation, MJ."

"Indeed," said Robin looking at the bowl before her with anticipation.

"It is one of my favorite summer time desserts. My mother used to make this for us on special occasions."

"Well let's see what it is," Dean said, picking up his spoon. We all began eating.

"What the … ?" Dean's nostrils flared as he bent his head over the bowl dipping within six inches of it. He stirred the contents, lifted his spoon a few times, examined the ingredients more closely, put one more spoonful in his mouth, and then let the spoon clatter as it fell out of his hand.

A laugh started in his belly and rose up to shake his whole being. "It's only rice, milk, and sugar!" he exclaimed. "This isn't a dessert. It is rice, milk and sugar. There isn't one redeeming thing about this concoction. Maybe it's a confabulation!"

I tried to tell him about how my mother made it so distinctive, and that it was a treat to me.

Robin attempted to interject patronizing solace, but Dean's reactions took center stage.

"What kind of mother would tell her child that a bowl of rice, milk, and sugar was something good. Or special!" he asked to empty air, pushing his bowl away with a flourish.

Choking back the tears, I removed the napkin from my lap, laid it to the right of my blue and white cone-shaped bowl, and put my spoon down on the smooth, soft surface. "Well, I know you have to get up early in the morning to teach," I announced as nonchalantly as possible, "so I'd better see you to the door."

The ploy worked. Within minutes they were gone. Their plethora of compliments on the main meal failed to move me, or allay my disappointment. Dean was still chuckling about dessert.

Cautiously, I placed my dessert in the refrigerator and emptied the contents of Robin and Dean's still full bowls down the garbage disposal. The routine of clearing the table and washing the rest of the dinner dishes almost went too quickly. Untying the waist straps of my seashell apron, I slipped it over my neck, and hung it on its designated hook.

Mom, Dad and I believed in angels and positive helper spirits. Part of our family lore was that whenever we were traveling, or simply away from each other, alive or beyond the veil, a bit of the spirits of the other family members were sitting on our shoulders. They were there to keep us company, to guide us, and be present for us. It was always permissible to commune with the spirits. We are, after all, half (or more) Irish.

"Okay, Mom, let's try this again," I said aloud. Carefully replacing my chilled dessert on the aluminum tray, with a fresh spoon and blue napkin on the side, and my royal blue iced tea glass, I carried it back out to the porch. That evening, I sat in silent communion

131

with the spirit of my mother in the chair beside me.

We shared a stunning sunset. No cloud bank interfered with the fiery ball's gradual descent as it appeared to sink into the ocean. With each whiff of cinnamon, and taste of vanilla, clove, nutmeg, brown sugar, and rice savor, I could see the pride in my mother's eyes serving it to me as a child.

Her delight at being able to sprinkle sugar in my dessert after the enforced rations of WWII. And spices! To *have* spices! Cinnamon and nutmeg, her favorites. To be able to have enough to eat so that there were leftovers. And to creatively use the leftover rice to make a treat; a dessert!

This was a joy of a woman who was birthed into a world on the brink of World War I, spent her first five years growing up in a world consumed by war, lost family and friends to the influenza pandemic of 1918 to 1920 and other diseases at a time when antibiotics were unknown, and endured the Great Depression during which my proud, stoic grandfather lost his once-thriving business, and their family home. A woman who slowly watched her mother lose her sanity after three of her babies died. A woman who suffered widowhood during the Second World War after my brother's father died in France, and then built a new life rising from the ashes.

Margaret Elizabeth Burrell Asman Koerper. This was the woman who rocked me to sleep every night, scratched my back, rubbed alcohol on my legs to quell my tears from wrenching growing pains, never left my side during illness, and held a cold wash cloth to my head when I was sick to my stomach. This was the woman, and these were the times I honored, with every bite of that simple dessert, whose substance goes far beyond ingredients and tastes that linger in my mouth.

As the essence of twilight transformed into the darkness of night, I watched the coastline take on ethereal, mystical contours shaped by twinkling lights. I took a deep breath and placed my empty bowl, spoon, and napkin back on the tray. "Thanks for the yummy treat, Mom, and this precious time together," I said aloud to the woman who gave me life and fed my soul, then, and now.

JOAN KOERPER

A Blink of an Eye

It had been a long drive that day going east on the I-94 through the Plains of North Dakota. I struggled to hold the steering wheel at a 45 degree angle to the left, driving into the north winds, just to stay on the road. Steady gale-force gusts slammed against the truck pushing it south. If you had seen the Highway Patrol car ahead of me, and my truck, from a chopper you would have declared us drunk—weaving, bobbing, and trying desperately not to be toppled and blown, vehicle and all, into the Badlands.

That's why I exited when I saw the sign for the Theodore Roosevelt National Park. Even at a standstill near the entrance to the Park, the truck rocked and swayed straining to buffer the high winds. But at least I could give my tired, stressed, arms and eyes a break.

The life-sized statue of the bison stood to the left of the entrance only a few feet from where we parked. The sculpture loomed over us. The average bison is, after all, about six feet tall and weighs around two-thousand pounds. If I looked straight at the statue I was staring at the bottom of the chest where the legs and chest joined. I had to angle my head, almost laying it on my left shoulder, to look out the driver's side window and peer skyward at the upper torso and head.

"Look at that, Spirit and Kitty," I said to my cats, traveling in their carriers, condo-style, on the passenger seat beside me. "What an amazing statue. Look how huge it is. To think the bison roamed this whole land at one time. Wow!"

I continued. "I wonder who did this sculpture. You'd think there would be a sign with the sculptor's name. We can really get a feel for their size. And it is so lifelike!"

Spirit twilled, which, in his language, means "Come play with me!"

"Hmmm," I mused.

I angled my head again and gazed up at the face of the statue. An eye blinked!

"Oh my God, Spirit! This isn't a statue! It's a real bison!"

Spirit twilled again, ready to play with his new friend outside our window.

I had heard how peaceful bison are which is why, of course, the species was driven to the brink of extinction, literally. I hoped the peaceful part was still true.

Angling my head again, this time straining, I detected a few hairs in his coat slightly ruffling, roused by the high winds. And the almost imperceptible twinges of his nostrils as he breathed.

I raised my eyes to his and they locked in. My breath caught. We spent some time in that space beyond words where the invisible threads that connect two manifestations of life merge into one.

Spirit twilled one last time and broke the silence. I moved into the rhythm of language and uttered a few phrases of affection to Mr. Bison followed by a fond farewell. Waving good-bye and whispering words of gratitude, the cats and I slowly pulled away from a chance encounter I'll never forget.

The Fire

The year was 1977. We were living in an apartment complex after a few months of living with my grandmother's brother, Uncle Louie, who had served in Korea and been stationed at March Air Force Base for many years. After several months of living with him and his family, it became clear that we had to find another place to live, if only temporarily, before we bought our own home the following year.

The apartment complex was built in the middle of a vast land tract that was plowed periodically. The rich deposits of red clay in the soil made it appear very reddish in color and it was a delight to go there and make little clay bowls out of it. All you had to do was add a little water or vast amounts of spit, as we sometimes did, to the dirt and it would congeal to form a nice soft substrate perfect for pottery making. The Riverside International Raceway was just a stone's throw away to the west side of the complex and we could hear the roar of the race cars during race events on the weekends.

A 13-year-old kid named Bill Gudino was my best friend at the time. He was two years older than me and he took me under his wing as a little brother when we met. We would hang out and do things like play football, ride our bikes and go exploring in the fields and sheltered tree lined arroyos near the complex. When the fields were freshly plowed, we would liberate giant cardboard refrigerator boxes from the trash bin, cut the end flaps off, and use them to tumble around inside on the dirt. It was a lot of fun and we sometimes had contests on who could go the fastest over a certain distance. We never got hurt though because the fields were very soft due to the constant plowing that was done to the land.

One day, on a particularly hot summer late afternoon, Bill told me he needed my help to do something top secret. Thinking this was an opportunity to do something fun and develop his trust in me, I instantly said yes and we left my apartment. I kept asking him what kind of top secret thing we were about to do, but he never answered my questions. He just continued telling me that no matter what it was, it was very important for me not to tell anyone about it, not even my

135

parents. It had to be kept top secret and he made me vow to never tell anyone about it. After I vowed that I would never tell anyone about it, we walked over towards the grassy field. A series of large rainstorms the previous month had turned the fields ablaze with local grasses and weeds, particularly tumble weeds since the fields hadn't been plowed yet. My thoughts began to speculate about what kind of secret he want to show me. Was it a dead body he wanted me to look at? Did he find a brief case full of mob money like we had sometimes joked about? Or, was it an entrance to a secret tunnel that led to an underground military bunker?

As my thoughts continued to race on what kind of secret it could be, he led me to an area in the field where some tumble weeds were clumped together. He crouched down under them and reached into his pocket. As I looked down, he said that we had to be very careful about anyone seeing us. He told me to block his body from field of view to which I complied. He continued by saying that after it was done, we had to go back home and never tell anyone about it, not even the cops.

"The cops?" I asked.

"Yes, even the cops." He replied.

He told me that under no circumstances was I to tell anyone that we had been together that day. He took out a book of matches from his pocket and began to light a match.

"Why are you a lighting a match?" I asked.

He looked up and grinned devilishly and reached into his other pocket and took out a small piece of paper.

"We're going to start a fire and become famous on the news," he said.

"Start a fire? I don't think that's a good idea." I replied.

I instinctively turned around and glanced back towards the apartment complex and the adjacent parking lot in the distance to see if anyone was watching us. When I turned back, he lit the small piece of paper on fire and tossed it into a clump of dried out tumble weeds in front of him. The flames licked wildly at the new found fuel source and began to grow in intensity. He stood up and said, "Don't be a chicken! When you go back home, you must not tell anyone what we did, understand?"

Before I could respond back, he took off running back

towards the apartment complex. As I stood there in complete astonishment of what had just happened, I hesitated for a moment, and then quickly reached down and grabbed a huge mound of soft clay red dirt and threw it on flames. After the fire was extinguished, I began to think about our friendship and how he had tricked me into taking part in something that was very dangerous. It was right then and there I made a vow to myself to never do anything I didn't want to do even if I thought they were my so-called best friend. Ironically, he moved out of the complex less than a month later and I never saw him again.

Frances J. Vasquez

La Llorona and the Gage Child
(The Legend of the Weeping Woman)

They say that the legend of *La Llorona*—the Weeping Woman is true. Many people in the Inland region swear she really exists. They wonder why she weeps, and why her spirit wanders all over the Continent, from Mexico and all over the Southwest looking for her *lost* children. There are many stories about *La Llorona* haunting the Santa Ana River and the Gage Canals. One local story took place back in 1893 when *La Llorona,* is said to have abducted a little girl while her father was attending an important meeting at the opulent Loring Opera House in Riverside.

The story of *La Llorona* is an ancient legend, passed on from generation to generation, of a tragic incident that began many centuries ago. It is a sad story of a young mother who drowned her own beloved two children. Yes, her OWN children! And she loved them, too! Loved them to death! What would drive a loving mother to drown her precious son and daughter? Innocent children who did nothing wrong, and adored their lovely mother … . Could it have been *corage*? Rage? Revenge … ? Or was she an insane monster?

Let me tell you the story of *La Llorona* and how this desperate, wandering spirit has terrified children and their parents for centuries. But, before I describe what happened in Riverside, I will explain how the legendary ghost story began in ancient Mexico—long before the explorations of Columbus, and way before the conquest by Cortes.

Over 600 years ago, a beautiful Aztec girl named *Mali* was married to a handsome warrior named *Potec*. The early Aztecs were a nomadic tribe that traveled up and down the *American* Continent, from as far North as present-day Oregon, to as far South as Central America.

Mali and *Potec* lived happily together with their two young children: a son and a daughter. *Mali* was most happy when they lived in the Central Valley of Mexico where there were plentiful turkeys,

138

fish, and abundant fruit to eat. She would become sad when *Potec* would leave them alone when he traveled to *el Norte* in search of tribute for the emperor.

One fateful day, *Potec* made an announcement that shook *Mali* to the core of her tender heart. *Potec* told her, *"Mujer, I am taking another wife. Tomorrow, I will come for my children at Daybreak. Have them ready for me."*

"No! No!" Mali cried out. *"Please, I beg you. Don't leave me! Don't take my life blood ... please don't take away my children! They are my precious jewels ..."*

Potec was not swayed by *Mali's* pleas. He told her, *"I have spoken, woman. Have the children ready when I return at Daybreak,"* and he walked away.

Mali was shocked! She was in anguish and beside herself. She began screaming and running around her hut in circles—she started pulling at her long hair—she didn't want to lose her children, and feared being left alone.

"Ay dioses! Gods of the Sun and the Stars; Goddess of Love and Motherhood, please help me," she pleaded desperately. *Mali's* children were more precious to her than all the jade and gold in the world.

She cried out in tormented screams, "ay, *mis hijos*—ay, ay, ay, ay, *mis hijos*!" She screamed until her voice was lost to mere guttural whimpers. She cried out, until nothing came out anymore. Silently, with tears streaming down her cheeks, *Mali* prepared a delicious supper for her children. She cooked their favorite meal of beans & chili with *nopalitos*. This time she added plump shrimps from a nearby lake. And, she grilled hot *tortillas de maiz*. Yes, a feast fit for royalty. The best for her precious blood ...

The children ate their supper with gusto, but *Mali* had no appetite for food. She could not stop thinking about the loss of her beloved children. It was like a nightmare. After supper, she donned her best *huipil*—the white one with the exotic *Quetzal* birds that she had painstakingly embroidered. She let down her long, lustrous black hair. The three went on an evening walk. The children loved those walks, especially when they sang joyful songs with their mother. Tonight, *Mali* felt no joy. She silently held their hands as they meandered toward the river.

The mother and children strolled along the banks of the river. *"Mis hijos,* my precious jewels, lets bathe in the warm waters," beckoned *Mali.* She and the children stepped into the shore of the gently flowing river. The children gleefully jumped up and down with their mother, and they waded towards the center until the three were in the deep.

Obsessed with dark thoughts of her husband taking her children away, and perhaps never to see them again, *Mali* grabbed them both swiftly by the nape of their little heads and pushed them under the water. She held her children down until they struggled no more ...

Suddenly, the sky turned an ominous dark color. Thunder rumbled loudly. Then, frightening lightning bolts struck the river! The normally gentle waters swirled in wild currents and swept away the children's bodies—away from *Mali's* grasp. The lifeless little bodies floated down the river.

Mali was jolted out of what seemed a daze. She was horrified to realize the horrific deed she had just committed. Frantic with remorse, she swam in the direction of the swift currents where she had last seen her little boy and girl get swept away. *"Ay, mis hijos!"* she cried. *"Dioses del cielo, quiero mis hijos!"* she wailed. *"Ay mis hijos; ay, ay!"*

Thereafter, for all eternity the weeping woman was condemned to search for her children. They say that *La Llorona's* ghost has abducted countless of children. She has been seen and heard along waterways all over the Americas innumerable times. Wailing, weeping out loud, *La Llorona* searches for her elusive children. Her search is unrelenting. Many children have disappeared, and many people swear that it was *La Llorona* who took them ...

Over the years, there have been reports of *La Llorona* sightings in Riverside, especially along the *Agua Mansa* area of South Colton where the Santa Ana River flows down from the San Bernardino mountains. Also, along the Gage Canals through Highgrove and the Inland region.

Back in the day, the Loring Opera House was the most lavish public place in Riverside to attend cultural events and see important people. Even in this luxurious building *La Llorona* wreaked havoc. It happened on April 22, 1893 when a group of prominent growers held a meeting to discuss important financial matters pertaining to the cit-

140

rus industry. Matthew Gage was one of those men at the meeting. Matthew, his wife Jane, and their four children immigrated to Riverside from Canada in 1881. His creation in 1886 of the Gage Canals, a water irrigation system, brought wealth and prosperity to local citrus growers, and of course to the Gage family.

The Gage's youngest daughter, Anna was abducted by *La Llorona*. It happened not too far from Downtown Riverside, near the then Seventh Street Bridge that crossed over the Santa Ana River into West Riverside. The river was swollen and quite beautiful due to the abundant rainfall. While Mr. Gage was tending to business at the Loring, Mrs. Gage took their two youngest children, 10-year old Robert and seven-year old Anna for a picnic on the banks of the river. Accompanying them was the Gage Canal "Mayordomo," Leonardo Vasquez who drove them in a large horse-drawn wagon. He planned to monitor the canal *gate heads* from the river to ensure effective water conveyance.

The day was particularly clear and delightful. After partaking of a lovely picnic lunch, Mrs. Gage and the children read and enjoyed a leisurely afternoon. *El Mayordomo* was busy with his work. Young Robert and little Anna soon became restless and asked to go play along the river bank. They skipped and ran happily along the river and played with the frogs and lizards that leaped and scampered through the Sage brush and tall sweet grass that flourished in the area.

Anna and Robert played "Hide-&-Seek" in a Sycamore grove. Then, Anna wandered off into a thick bushy area at the river's edge. In the river, she saw a strange, yet pretty lady with long dark hair wearing a white dress. She sang out to Anna—beckoning her with her hands to join her in the water. Anna didn't know who she was, but was mesmerized by the lady's cooing voice. Trance-like, Anna stepped into the river and waded towards the out-stretched arms of the lady. The lady took Anna into her arms, turned around and began to wade deeper toward the river's center.

Meanwhile, Jane Gage was frightened to learn that her little Anna had separated from her brother and went missing. *El Mayordomo* responded to Mrs. Gage's anguished cries and sent one of his sons to fetch Mr. Gage, who was still in a meeting at the Loring. Then, *El Mayordomo* ran in the direction that Robert told him he had last seen his little sister.

A spiritual man, *El Mayordomo* prayed for God's divine intervention to help find Anna. He gathered a bundle of Sacred Sage to smudge away negativity in the area. Holding the Sage as a torch, he ran like an Olympian toward the river. He saw his worst fear: *La Llorona* had taken Anna! There they were, in the river. He jumped in and swam toward them as fast as a Dolphin, and when he approached *La Llorona*, he swiftly flung his Rosary beads over her head. *La Llorona* was immobilized by the Holy beads, and *El Mayordomo* quickly snatched Anna away from her. He swarm with the child safely in his arm to the river side—never looking back. By that time, Mr. Gage had arrived to the river's edge and both parents were gratified and overjoyed to see their daughter was safely rescued by Mr. Vasquez. Thankfully, Anna didn't remember anything about the *La Llorona* incident.

In appreciation for his courage and quick thinking, Leonardo Vasquez, *El Mayordomo* was honored by the Mayor of Riverside. The City also, dedicated a street in his name, "Vasquez Place." The Gage family hosted a huge barbecue at Fairmount Park, and the entire city celebrated Mr. Vasquez' heroic and selfless actions to save little Anna from the snares of *La Llorona*.

It is no wonder that for years and years, parents, especially Hispanic parents have warned their children not to go out alone at night for fear that *La Llorona* might snatch them for her own. These fears are particularly ominous in places like Riverside which have abundant lakes, canals, and a river. Whether an insane or desperate wondering spirit, *La Llorona* continues her relentless quest to find her children—or anyone else's children.

Frances J. Vasquez

"El Chueco"

Hijole! *Chueco* was tough! Tough to the core. It took a heck of a long time to cook the *gallo* (rooster) for the soup I was making for dinner. Over and over again, I tested the meat with a fork for doneness. The tines wouldn't budge! Not one bit, even after an hour of simmering the fowl's body parts. I began to feel nervous, as it was starting to get late for preparing dinner.

They say that you're not supposed to add raw vegetables to the soup stock until the meat is almost tender, otherwise the vegetables get too mushy. So, every 15 minutes, I tried poking a piece of that chicken. That damned *gallo* wouldn't give! Even in soup *Chueco* was contrary.

Vintage recipes for homemade chicken soup state that stewing hens make the most flavorful chicken soup stock. Back in the day, markets offered wider varieties of fresh chicken to select from. Stewing hens were cheaper than fryers. They're also tougher because the hens were too old to lay anymore eggs. I remember when *Stater Bros.* sold stewing hens for only 19 cents a pound compared to fryers, which sold for 39 cents a pound. Being a young and frugal homemaker, I once purchased a stewing hen to make homemade chicken soup. Never again, I thought. It took too long to simmer the stewing hen to make the meat tender enough for my small son to eat. Thereafter, it became standard practice for me to buy fryer chickens even for home cooked chicken soup.

When my three sons were little we kept a few chickens in our small back yard. Our rationale was that the daily chore of feeding and caring for animals would instill in our sons some valuable life-long lessons in responsibility. Also, the eggs that backyard chickens produced would be superior in flavor and quality than the store-bought eggs. So, we purchased a half-dozen baby chicks, including *Rhode Island Reds* for a daily supply of tasty brown eggs.

We kept the little chicks in a rabbit hutch, which we suspended onto our redwood fence above the ground in our backyard. Being ecologically-minded, we used their droppings for a worm bed and fer-

143

tilizer for our vegetable garden. When the chickens grew bigger, we let them out of their cage occasionally to let them to sunbathe and range freely on the ground for worms, insects, and seeds. One of the so called *chicks* grew up to be a huge, white rooster with a bright red crooked comb which crowned the top of his head. The boys named him "Chueco," or crooked. To be sure, his name was a foreshadowing of what he was to become.

One beautiful Spring morning, I sent the two older boys, Leonard and Mark out to play in the backyard while I busied myself with household chores and tended to our toddler, Andy. Suddenly, with a loud clamor, the two boys burst into the kitchen, wide-eyed with terrified looks on their faces.

"Mommy, mommy! *Chueco's* chasing us!" They both shouted excitedly. "He keeps trying to bite us! He's mean! We don't want to be out there anymore!"

"Hmm," I thought, "what could be so terrifying about an innocent rooster? The boys just want an excuse to come inside and watch TV," I surmised.

So, I quickly responded, "oh, come on, *love bugs*" (as I liked to call my sons back then), "he's just a harmless rooster ... how can he hurt you? Come on, let's go back outside and play."

Unable to convince me of *Chueco's* torments, Leonard and Mark reluctantly went outside through the kitchen door that leads to our garage. I noticed that they picked up some garden tools we kept in the garage. They carried them like weapons in their hands: one boy held a shovel and the other one held a rake. They made their way to the backyard—with *weapons* in hand to defend themselves against the bully rooster.

Weeks later, while home alone, I decided to prepare the soil in a backyard brick planter to plant seeds for a vegetable garden. I put on a pair of comfortable Bermuda shorts and an old cotton top and went out to work in the garden. Because the planter was only two bricks high, I was bent over on my knees, carefully turning and loosening the soil with a hand trowel. I was quietly working the rich sandy loam soil Arlington is blessed with. Suddenly, from behind me, I heard *Chueco* start flapping his immense wings. He lunged towards me and snapped me hard on a portion of the exposed back of my waist. He had attacked me without any provocation! I was minding

144

my own business … just like my boys had done so many times.

Cabron Chueco! "The boys were right," I thought. "He's one mean rooster." Right then and there, I was determined that *Chueco* was cooked … I decided to make soup out of that mean *gallo*. But, it was no easy task to serve him for a family meal. He was a tough, fighting rooster to the end. And the soup, how did it taste? I don't know. I couldn't eat it … him. Did *Chueco* win his last battle after all?

The Other California Migrants

I wish I had learned how to make lefse.

My grandmother, mother and aunts would pick a day just before Christmas or Thanksgiving to get together and churn out lefse (lef-sa) for our holiday meal. The pounds and pounds of potatoes would already be boiled; one aunt would be mashing the potatoes, another mixing them into other ingredients to form a dough, while yet another would be using a narrowly grooved rolling pin to roll the dough into a thin, plate-sized tortilla-like pancake. Perhaps it would be my grandma, standing at the griddle turning the lefse with a long wooden stick, not flat or quite as long as a yardstick. We children would eagerly await a sample of lefse, spread it with butter and sprinkle it with sugar, roll it up and savor every bite.

The kitchen was filled with warmth from the making and turning of the lefse and the camaraderie of the women of the family as they visited while they carried on a tradition that came from my grandfather's Swedish roots and the influence of the many other Scandinavians from Norway and Sweden who were their friends, neighbors and fellow parishioners. These immigrants homesteaded in Minnesota and the Dakotas, a climate similar to what they left behind in the "old country" when they came to America.

My grandparents, Anje and Alex Norton, started their married life in a sod house built from the dirt of the South Dakota prairie. Held together by thick prairie grasses, blocks of dirt were cut from the soil and used to build homes. It was the only material available in abundance that the homesteaders could afford for building their homes until the railroad could come through with lumber and other supplies. Even then, many of the homesteaders would be lucky if they could afford a door or windows for their home—but they were better off than some who lived in shelters more primitive than sod houses.

My grandmother's family, of Dutch ancestry, had come north from Kentucky to settle near Lodgepole, South Dakota, just a few miles from the border with North Dakota. My grandfather emigrated from Sweden through Ellis Island and also ended up at the sparsely

146

settled area. Here, the government offered free land to those who would be willing to improve their claim and make it their home.

One day, as family legend goes, my grandfather was roofing a barn when he saw my grandmother pass by in a horse-drawn wagon. He said, "That's the woman I am going to marry."

And he did.

But, life was harsh on the prairie. The winters were bitter cold; summers were hot and dry and the wind almost always blew, no matter the season. Grasshoppers or hail could wipe out the entire work of a planting season—and thus, the income for the year. Those who homesteaded and stayed had to be a hardy lot, depending on family and neighbors to make it through those early years. Women helped one another through childbirths; many of these women did not survive the rigors of multiple childbirths or illnesses such as pneumonia, leaving their husbands with small children to raise or farm out to relatives. My mother, the first of nine children, was born in the sod house. Two of her sisters died in infancy and their small, white, grave markers, still etched with their names and dates of birth and death, stand in the windswept cemetery next to the tiny Lodgepole Lutheran Church that was so central to the Norton family in those early years.

The children of homesteaders attended one-room schools on the prairie with a single teacher for all eight grades. The teacher had many responsibilities, including tending to the pot-bellied stove, so necessary for warmth during the winter months. If the school was too far away to walk, children might arrive by horseback, often two or three riding bareback on one horse. One time, a fierce blizzard—a combination of severe wind and snow—was on its way and my grandfather raced to the school with a horse and sled to bring his children home before it hit. Blizzards could be deadly to livestock as well as to pioneer families; to be stranded in a blizzard could mean sure death.

But it wasn't all hard times. There were dances and Ladies' Aid meetings and barn raisings and quilting bees. Women would spend hours preparing food on their wood cook stoves and wagons would be laden with children and food as people arrived to an event from far and wide. Men played cards or horseshoes or perhaps even musical instruments. Horse-drawn wagons soon gave way to cars and trucks with skinny tires and hand-cranked starters. Sod houses were

147

replaced with "real" houses made of lumber. My grandparents, who did not farm but raised sheep, ultimately built what was, for that time, a very nice farmhouse; it still stands today, its wooden floors still intact and beautiful.

At some point, my grandmother's parents, Susie and John Harm Beld, moved to Riverside, California. From the stories I have heard, I picture them traveling much like the Joads did when they left Oklahoma during the Dust Bowl in John Steinbeck's novel, *The Grapes of Wrath*. Henry Fonda starred in the black and white movie that followed. In it, the Joad family heads for California, packing all of their earthly goods on their old cars and trucks. Some of the family members sat on chairs on the beds of the trucks, surrounded by belongings as they made their way west. The overload would be piled on fenders and tops of the vehicles and hanging along the sides, similar to the way the earlier pioneers headed west in their covered wagons.

I don't know why Riverside was chosen by the Belds and their westward move did not result in the types of prejudice that some Californians felt toward "Okies" from Oklahoma like the Joads. One of my uncles, who had less than twenty dollars in his pocket when he and my aunt left Dakota, became a custodian at the museum in Riverside; another became a deputy sheriff.

Around 1947, my grandparents sold everything at a farm auction and retired to Riverside. After first living on Prospect Avenue in a house that was later demolished for the freeway, Grandma and Grandpa moved to 3643 Eucalyptus Avenue, directly across from Longfellow Elementary School and just a block away from Grandma's mother and sister. Here, they continued many of their frugal ways, ways that were deeply ingrained in them from living through hard times. They were extremely frugal with their money— and with water. They never took it for granted.

Grandma did her laundry on the back porch of the Eucalyptus house where she still made her own lye laundry soap. I don't know the recipe for that, either—I just remember, after making it, she would cut the solid cake-size layer of hard white soap into bars, then grate them by hand on a kitchen grater. The grated soap came out in creamy curls that would more easily dissolve as her wringer washer agitated the wash water. Then she would rinse the laundry in two different tin tubs

148

and hang it on the line to dry in the California sunshine. This must have seemed like a little slice of heaven after doing laundry for a family of nine, first hauling water to fill tin washtubs, then scrubbing the clothing and other laundry against the rough surface of a washboard before hanging it on the clothesline where the wind would whip it around, making it smell deliciously clean and fresh.

Grandpa kept chickens in a fenced off section in the very back of their deep back yard. The chickens would get all of the table scraps and vegetable peels. Coffee grounds were put on plants which were sometimes watered with dishwater. Grandma made most of her own clothes and would proudly announce what a particular dress might have cost her.

"Would you believe I made this for two dollars and thirty-five cents?" she would ask. She would always look tall and elegant, especially when she went to church. They were members of Eden Lutheran Church when it was still a small church, before the new one was built on Brockton Avenue near Central Middle School.

About a half block from their house, there was a tiny store on the corner. The store had most likely been converted from a garage built for a Model T-sized car. It jutted out from the house where its owners, Bill and Erny, lived. Bill was a thin, sad and lonely looking man and Erny had a short, curly fluff of orange-ish red hair and bright red lipstick. Erny would sit for hours at my grandma and grandpa's dining room table, playing cards with my grandpa, a constant cigarette dangling from her lips, a cloud of blue smoke hovering over the cards. Bill kept a cigar box with postage stamps and I'm sure I was one of his best stamp customers. I think he liked seeing me come through the wooden screen door; he'd open the cigar box, knowing that was what I was there for, give me my stamps and put the money in the box before placing it back under the counter.

In those early California years, several of my mother's sisters and many of her Beld cousins lived in the Riverside and Rubidoux area. Her cousin, Lydia Beld Chaires, helped my mother find a job when we arrived in California to stay in 1957. We had Norton family get-togethers, often having tacos at my aunt and uncle's on Fifth Street, next to the railroad tracks. On holidays, I looked forward to lefse but not lutefisk, another traditional Swedish dish. What I know about lutefisk is that it is a disgustingly smelly, white, gelatinous blob of fish that my grandpa and uncle ate with lots of butter on it. They bought it at some place on North Main Street in Riverside and they had to order it several days in advance because it went through some special process with water and lye. It seems they brought it home in a bucket of water. I never watched them cook it. I can't say that I have any regrets about not learning how to fix lutefisk!

Not long before their 50th anniversary, Grandma had a stroke and this once proud, straight-standing woman was hunched and broken, hardly able to feed herself, so different from the strong prairie woman who tended to a large family or made dinner for large groups of people. She, who was once so prim and proper, had not a shred of dignity left as others had to tend to her most basic, personal needs, so different from the strong woman who sheltered neighbors stranded by a snowstorm or advised a young girl who had lost her mother. About a year after my grandmother died, on a hot August day, my frugal-as-ever 82-year-old grandfather walked to the day-old bakery on Eighth Street to buy a loaf of bread. That night, he died in his sleep.

But I'm glad they were able to live an easier life in California after those hard first years in Dakota. It must have been like a miracle for them to have sunshine most of the year, to be able to pluck an apricot, still warm from the sun, right from the tree and enjoy its juicy goodness, to turn on the faucet and have hot, running water.

Here, I have written about the hardships and the harsh weather of the Dakotas—but there is great beauty and wonder to be found in the landscape there—and yes, the weather, too. The people who have lived there for years have resilience and kindness and look out for one another to this day; if you are stranded on a roadside, for example, nearly anyone who happens by would be willing to help you.

I don't know what my grandfather's life was like in Sweden. I'm not sure what gave him the courage to cross the ocean on a large ship and come to a new country and learn the language and never ask for anything. There was no free medical care, no welfare or even Social Security. It is important to tell their story because I think people tend to forget about these other, earlier migrants to California, people like my grandparents, who endured extremely harsh conditions before they ever arrived here.

And now, back to the lefse. I thought I was observant. I

150

thought I listened. But, in reality, I didn't. There are so many unanswered questions for me about my heritage. I wish I had asked more, listened more. I wish I had taken a post in the kitchen, mashing or kneading or rolling or turning, dusted with flour amid the chatter of loved ones while I learned how to make lefse.

And now, there is no one left to teach me. Oh, I can go on the Internet for recipes and instructions and even a $200 lefse-making kit—but it just isn't the same.

I wish I had learned how to make lefse.

Contributor Biographies

Donna Buck is a writer who writes fiction, essays, and poetry, including free verse and Japanese short form poetry, especially haibun and tanka prose. She has been published in several online and print journals, such as *Avocet, Haibun Today, Contemporary Haibun Online, Kernels, Skylark* (upcoming issue), *Prune Juice* (upcoming) and *Survivors Review.*

Celena Diana Bumpus, BA, AODA, is CEO of three publishing houses, including Islands for Writers Publishing. Her poetry collection *Confessions: Laguna Poets Series #118* is part of the esteemed Laguna Poets Series (The Inevitable Press, 1998). Her poetry has appeared in more than five anthologies and literary journals. Her personal essay will appear in the upcoming book *Street Lit: Representing The Urban Landscape Edited* by Keenan Norris (Scarecrow Press, 2014). She teaches poetry, fiction, and nonfiction at the Janet Goeske Senior Center in Riverside, CA. Celena has featured as a performing poet for the last 20 years in venues throughout Southern California. She co-hosts "Dreams within the Ocean Literary Venue" at Shades of Afrika in Corona, CA, where she publishes four free copies of books for her featured readers. Celena also mentors a young author in writing through her "Lake River Moon" project. Her website is www.oceanmoonspirit.blogspot.com.

Brutus Chieftain is the pen name for John Bender, Metro editor of the *Press-Enterprise*, and co-founder of the guerrilla poetry performance troupe, Poets in Distress. Brutus lives in Moreno Valley with his wife and two sons. Brutus continues to perform with the Poets in Distress, as he has for the past three decades. At work, John Bender co-hosts the Inlandia Literary Journeys video program and assists with the weekly Inlandia print column and daily Inlandia blog. He is a Cal Poly Pomona graduate.

Michael J. Cluff is a full-time English Composition, Critical Thinking and Creative Writing professor at Norco College. He has recently been published in *Phantom Seed, Inlandia: A Literary Journey, The Sand Canyon Review, The Toucan, Medusa's Kitchen, Epiphany*, and *Locust* poetry magazines and flash fiction at *Eskimopigirl*. His ninth poetry book *Elegant Worry* was published by Palabra Press in 2011.

Deenaz P. Coachbuilder has been a resident of the Riverside area since 1981. She received a Doctorate in Theater Arts from Brigham Young University, an M.S. in Communicative Disorders from Utah State, an M.A. and B.A from Bombay University in English Literature and Language. Deenaz is a retired school principal, and professor in Special Education at California State University, San Bernardino, past president of Committee for Community Action and Environmental Justice and India Association of the Inland Empire, and a consultant in Speech Pathology. Deenaz is actively involved in the Zoroastrian Association of California and is writing a poem on the birth and evolution of the religion and its adherents, extending to the modern period. Most recently, her poems have appeared in *The Sun Runner, Sugar Mule Literary Magazine*, and *Parsiana*. Deenaz received President Obama's Volunteer Service Award in February 2011. Deenaz looks forward to sharing her book of poems, *Imperfect Fragments* with her friends and writers this December.

Carlos E. Cortés is Professor Emeritus of History at the University of California, Riverside. His most recent book is his autobiography, *Rose Hill: An Intermarriage before Its Time* (Berkeley, CA: Heyday, 2012). Cortés is general editor of *Multicultural America: A Multimedia Encyclopedia* (Sage, 2013), Scholar-in-Residence with Univision Communications, and Creative/Cultural Advisor for Nickelodeon's Peabody-award-winning children's television series, *Dora the Explorer*, and its sequel, *Go, Diego, Go!*, for which he received the 2009 NAACP Image Award. He also travels the country performing his one-person autobiographical play, *A Conversation with Alana: One Boy's Multicultural Rite of Passage*, while he co-wrote the book and lyrics for the musical, *We Are Not Alone: Tomás Rivera – A Musical Narrative*, which premiered in 2011.

154

Laurel V. Cortés went to Mexico City alone at age 17 to attend the University of Mexico. The experience changed her life and, after majoring in Spanish and minoring in Comparative Literature at San Diego State University, she worked for 28 years at the University of California, Riverside, in—guess what?—the Department of Literatures and Languages. The job perfectly suited her interests, and it's fun now to do a bit of writing on her own.

Donald Dietz is a retired Industrial Arts Teacher with a MA degree in Industrial Education and Counseling. In retirement he has developed several hobbies. During the time spent in Idyllwild he enjoys the Inlandia workshops where he has been encouraged to write. In his spare time he has written several poems and stories which have been inspired while hiking on the trails around Idyllwild. He is also a well known stained glass artist with works sold throughout the United States and Canada.

Myra Dutton is the author of *Healing Ground: A Visionary Union of Earth and Spirit*, which was a 2004 Narcissus Book Award finalist, recognized as one of 2003's "Top Ten Books" by *Shutterbug Magazine*, and was a 2006's "Ten Books We Love" selection by *Inland Empire Magazine*. She was interviewed on NPR's "Environmental Directions Radio" in October 2005 and was a featured poet on the "Tree of Life" special for the PBS Emmy Award-winning program, *Eco-News* in December 2006. She jointly leads the Idyllwild Inlandia Institute Creative Writing Workshop with Jean Waggoner.

Nan Friedley is a retired special education teacher transplanted from Indiana some 28 years ago. She taught in Fontana, the CA School for the Deaf in Riverside, and most recently in Moreno Valley. Now, she is trying her hand at writing with the help of the good people at Inlandia.

Françoise Frigola, a regular attendee of the Idyllwild Inlandia workshop, was born and raised in France. She writes spontaneously, often on current social issues. With an MA in transpersonal psychology she sees the astrological chart as a map of the person's psyche. For several years, she wrote a column on *Counseling Astrology* in Aspect magazine. She has a BS in Computer science and business administration and over 45 years of experience as a computer consultant. She is also an internationally exhibited and collected artist.

David Calvin Gogerty is an economist with a Stanford Bachelor's and Master's whose professional work is for private clients on problems of risk analysis. He is a co-author of articles in peer-reviewed journals in economics and operations research. He and his wife live in Idyllwild.

Michelle Gonzalez has lived in Riverside most of her life. She received her bachelors degree from UCR and also holds and MFA in creative writing from National University. Recently, she has also published two book of poems and has been an active participant in the Inlandia Workshops.

Marie Griffiths, a former registered nurse and English instructor, is retired and lives with her husband, Garry, in Fontana, California. A chronic "late bloomer," Marie began a liberal arts education in middle age, ultimately earning a Ph.D. from UCR in 1999. Still a neophyte in the realm of creative writing, she continues to hone her craft by composing short stories and poems. She is a proud member of the Inland Empire branch of the California Writers' Club.

Anita Harmon was born in London at the end of WWII. She studied at the Lycée Francais de Londres, and went on to become an improvisational actress on the London stage. At the same time she went back to school to study psychology, gained her degree, and as well as having a private practice for many years, she worked in the business community, teaching communication skill. Now retired, Anita Harmon lives in California and writes poetry and nonfiction.

Joan (MJ) Koerper is the author of *Threaded Hoops: Poems, Tracy Tackles Responsibility*, and co-author of the on-going series *The Adventures of Sage, the Super-Service Dog* with her Husky-Shepherd, All-American dog, Sage, now available on Amazon.com. MJ has published poetry, creative nonfiction, memoir, fiction, nonfiction, a one-woman play, and radio, video, and audiotape scripts for adults and children. She earned her Ph.D. in Humanities in the Writing, Consciousness and Creativity Program from the California Institute of Integral Studies, San Francisco, CA, her Master of Social Work degree from San Diego State University, and her B.A. from Michigan State University.

Richard M. Mozeleski is a retired landscape designer. He has been married to his wife Diane for 22 years, and is the father of Ian Mozeleski, a college basketball player. Richard has coached local basketball and baseball players for the past decade and took up writing and theater after moving to Idyllwild. Richard also does a ministry feeding the homeless.

Marsha Schuh and her husband Dave are currently remodeling the 88-year-old home in Ontario that they moved into as a young couple. She teaches English at CSUSB and is working on a collection of poems—inspired by her early morning walks—about Ontario and its history. Marsha's poetry has appeared in literary journals such as *Pacific Review, Badlands, The Sand Canyon Review, Shuf* and *Inlandia: A Literary Journey*.

Mike Sleboda has been a member of the Inlandia Creative Writing program since 2009 and has been published in *Slouching Towards Mt. Rubidoux Manor* and *2011 Writing from Inlandia*. He is currently a volunteer for the Inlandia Institute and earned his B.A. degree in Communications from Cal State University San Bernardino. He plans to pursue a career in TV/film production.

David Stone spent most of his childhood on his family's farm in Waverly, Pennsylvania. He is a seventh generation descendent from the founder of Waverly. David earned a Bachelors in English from Atlantic Union College and a Masters in English from La Sierra University. He has taught various courses in literature, writing, and ESL to high school and college students in Arkansas, California, Florida, Massachusetts, Pennsylvania, and Beijing, China. He currently teaches at Loma Linda Academy. David enjoys cooking, reading, and exploring nature with his wife and two children. His poems have appeared most recently in the online literary publications *Identity Theory* and *Shuf*.

Frances J. Vasquez resides in Riverside amid abundant citrus and guava trees. She has a diverse background in public service, and was the Executive Director (and CEO) of Other Cultures, Inc., an international student exchange program specializing in exchanges between Mexico, Central America, Canada, and the U.S. She attended local schools and graduated with BS and MBA degrees from the University of California, Riverside. An aficionada of the arts, Frances enjoys organizing and attending cultural events.

Jean Waggoner teaches English/English as a Second Language at several community colleges in Riverside County. She serves as one of Inlandia's Idyllwild workshop leaders with Myra Dutton and as an officer of the California Part-time Faculty Association. Her work has appeared in national and regional publications, including peer-reviewed journals and poetry blogs. In 2011 Jean and co-author Douglas Snow published *The Freeway Flier and the Life of the Mind*, a book that explores the challenges of creating while teaching.

Mae Wagner has written a column for her home town newspaper in North Dakota for the past six years. In the process, she has learned much about the early homesteaders who settled in that area. In 1957 her mother brought Mae and her sister to Riverside, California, to live where she often lived with her grandparents. Mae is fortunate to have a rich store of memories to draw upon for writing—not only from her Dakota roots but from her many years in the Inland Empire as well. Her essays have been published on the *Press-Enterprise*'s op-ed page on topics such as world-famous woodworker Sam Maloof and the Stringfellow Acid Pits. She has been a newspaper reporter/photographer for the *Chino Champion* and the Riverside Chamber of Commerce. She took her first class at Riverside City College in 1968 and graduated with honors 20 years later from Cal State San Bernardino. After jumping through ever-additional hoops, she became a teacher at the age of 50, first teaching in a teen mother program and later at a Continuation High School until the age of 65. She is a mother of three, grandmother of seven and great-grandmother of two. She currently lives in Redlands, California, with her husband, Alex, and the world's sweetest dog, Sophie.

About the Inlandia Institute

The Inlandia Institute is a regional non-profit literary center. We seek to bring focus to the richness of the literary enterprise that has existed in this region for ages. The mission of the Inlandia Institute is to recognize, support and expand literary activity in all of its forms through community programs in the Inland Empire, thereby deepening people's awareness, understanding, and appreciation of this unique, complex and creatively vibrant region.

The Institute publishes high quality regional writing in print and electronic form including books published in partnership with Heyday under the Inlandia Institute imprint as well as: Writing From Inlandia: Work of the Inlandia Creative Writing Workshops; the online literary journal, Inlandia: A Literary Journey; and, starting the winter of 2011, books directly under the Inlandia imprint, including Dos Chiles/Two Chilies, a children's chapter book by Julianna Cruz.

Inlandia presents free public literary programming featuring authors who live in, work in, and/or write about Inland Southern California. We also provide Creative Literacy Programs for children and youth and hold creative writing workshops for teens and adults.

To learn more about the Inlandia Institute please visit our website at InlandiaInstitute.org.

OTHER INLANDIA PUBLICATIONS